Small Town Arrival
Allie Harrison

www.allieharrison.com

Publisher's Note: This is a work of fiction. Names, characters, places, and incidents are a product of the author's imagination. Locales and public names are sometimes used for atmospheric purposes. Any resemblance to actual people, living or dead, or to businesses, companies, events, institutions, or locales is completely coincidental.

Book Layout © 2017 BookDesignTemplates.com[1]

Small Town Arrival/ Allie Harrison.—1st ed.

ISBN 978-1-7375784-9-9

---

1.   http://www.bookdesigntemplates.com/

To Andrea Miles Rhodes, Thank You

Dear Reader,

Welcome back to Mossy Point. Let me introduce you to the newest detective of the Mossy Point Police Department, Detective Tony Grayson. In 2022, I had the wonderful opportunity to join a talented group of authors and be included in several anthologies published by AMR. It was through these anthologies that I became an International Best-Selling Author. The first short story of this book, Small Town Elf was published in an anthology entitled Christmas Wish, released in December, 2023. The second story, Small Town Nightmare, was due to be published in April, 2024, in Whispers in the Shadows, but was canceled when unfortunately, Andrea Miles Rhodes passed away unexpectedly in March, 2024. The third story here, Small Town Urban Legend, was slotted for a historical horror anthology which was scheduled for release October, 2024, The Haunting of Devlin Mansion. This was also canceled. However, I wanted you, loyal reader, to meet Detective Grayson, as you will see him again in an upcoming release, Small Town Haunting.

Until then, happy reading.

Allie

Contents

Small Town Elf – 4

Small Town Nightmare – 34

Small Town Urban Legend – 79

Small Town Elf

In a USPS delivered envelope marked to Detective Tony Grayson, Personal and Confidential:

December 1

Dear Detective Grayson,

I am writing this short note to advise you your Christmas wish has been granted. I saw you two weeks ago on the local news stating that your only Christmas wish for this year would be that the Red Scarf Rapist would be stopped and brought to justice. Let me assure you, he has.

I want to say first and foremost that granting your Christmas wish wasn't what I planned or even remotely considered. I went to a Christmas party and had too many glasses of Christmas cheer, and I thought I'd better not drive. The Uber wait was almost an hour so I climbed into the backseat of a nearby cab.

The next thing I know, I'm waking up on the concrete floor in this cold, dank, warehouse-type place. It's lit up like an operating room and the lights hurt my eyes. My wrists are bound with plastic zip ties. My pants are wet, and I stink like pee. There's a man watching me. His smile makes me colder. He said he's happy I'm awake, finally, and when I ask, he tells me I've been out for over twenty hours. No wonder I feel like I've been run down by a truck, I thought. My stomach grumbled, my throat burned, and my body hurt all over. I had the impression by my position he'd dragged me to my present location and simply dropped me.

The place smelled like rubber and motor oil. I also had the faint lingering odor of coffee in my nose. The man held a cup in his hand, and I had the impression he'd held it under my nose so the smell of coffee helped wake me up. He explained to me he'd tasered me. He reprimanded me for drinking so much and partying. He called me a slut.

By then, I knew who he was, but he explained it to me anyway. He said it was his job to rid the world of sluts like me. That women were supposed to be married by the time they reached my age, and they were

4

supposed to be obedient and submissive to their husbands. My duty was to bear children and care for a family. Since he saw no ring on my finger, I was past my prime. My partying and drinking and evident flirting revealed me to be a 'loose' woman. He said he was there to judge me first and deal out what he felt was an appropriate punishment. He said he had a new red scarf just waiting for me so I could go to my ultimate judgement. He said first he was going to give me a 'scrubbing' shower to clean me on the outside. He was then going to make me watch while he burned 'my life away' which he explained was the burning of my clothes. He said he would soon have the fire in the incinerator going.

He told me he'd judged eighteen other sinning women like me. The news only reported the Red-Scarf Rapist to have had six victims, so somewhere along the line, Detective, you're off by twelve. But maybe that's just how the new math works.

He became angry at the idea I wasn't begging or pleading for my life, pleading for him to just let me go. I wasn't even crying or looking scared. He said I should be scared when I was standing before my judge. Inside I was shaking with terror, I assure you, but I wasn't about to give him an inch of satisfaction. I stared at him as he stared at me. I also looked around. The large room was filled with make-shift torture devices, but I'll bet you know that. You haven't revealed to the press the actual way some of these victims have died, but I'll bet they were all tortured in various ways. There were ropes connected to the ceiling and large hooks that looked like meat hooks you'd see in movies. There were boxes of gloves, tools, knives, other instruments I didn't recognize. There was a hose coiled on the floor.

I don't want to die, but I sure as hell didn't want to die there in that cold place in tortured pain. I didn't want to lie on that contraption that looked like it would stretch me until one of my feet snapped off.

There were dried blood spots in various places on the floor. I was terrified, but not so much of him actually. I was terrified my blood would join all that other blood and then just dry up into a spot on the floor. I was terrified that by that time the next day you'd be looking at my naked, dead body and a bunch of cops munching donuts and a photographer would be looking at me and studying me like a bug under a microscope. I was terrified my mother would be opening her door to a stranger who would tell her, her daughter was dead. I was terrified I would become number nineteen when you thought I was lucky number seven.

But I only stared at him and worked to keep my terror hidden despite the way my heart raced and pounded in my chest. My staring at him made him angry. He told me he was going to go start the incinerator and make himself a sandwich to keep up his strength for the upcoming festivities.

I angered him further by asking him what kind of sandwich. I told him pastrami was my favorite. With Swiss cheese and mustard with pickles. He kicked me in the gut as I lay there on the floor. He said when he returned, he expected more respect and obedience. He expected to see remorse for all my whorish ways. And he wanted to see my fear. He went out a door at the end of the room.

Now, a bit of history here, Detective. All my life, people have underestimated me. I don't know if it's because of my size or the color of my hair or the simple fact I have a vagina instead of testicles or what, and it has, in the past, always pissed me off. It didn't this time. I'm glad he underestimated me. As soon as he was gone, I got to work. You see, my daddy, didn't raise a dummy. Every joint in my body hurt, but I forced myself to move. I thought I could defend myself even with my wrists bound with a zip tie, but I thought I'd better use every advantage available. I made quick work of using my shoe lace, even though my fingers were stiff and cold. My purse that I'd had across my chest from one shoulder to my other hip when I climbed into the cab was thrown on the floor nearby. I grabbed it and opened it. Obviously, my kidnapper hadn't bothered to look inside or if he had he mistook the flashlight in there for nothing more than that—just a flashlight. It is just a flashlight, and a taser. By the time I heard the sounds of his whistling approaching—he sounded so lighthearted and happy, I thought I might puke—I was waiting for him next to the door. I even managed to put on a pair of his disposable gloves because I wanted to touch nothing of his in this horrid place with my bare skin. And I gave him exactly what he gave me, a taser jolt to the throat. He hit the floor with a slap and, like me, wet his pants. If I didn't care about having evidence of being in this place with him and I had my phone, I would have taken a picture.

His look of shock and surprise—unless it was just the taser—was so satisfying. The way his head smacked to the concrete was equally as satisfying. I had never used that taser and thought I might contact the company to thank them for how well it worked.

I quickly looked into the area beyond him, found it was a small kitchen and bathroom and we were alone. I didn't bother wasting time binding his hands. I know how to get out of that, maybe so did he.

He'd carried a knife in with him. It wasn't some small steak knife he'd use to cut his sandwich in half. It was one of those survival things you'd want if you were shipwrecked on a deserted island, big enough to skin a wild boar. It even had little saw teeth to cut tree branches so you could make a fire and roast your boar after you skinned it.

I'll be damned, but he fell on his knife. He fell on his knife five times. I hate when stupid people do stupid shit like that, but, well, it does happen. Before I could even attempt to call for help for him—which, of course, I couldn't at that moment. I didn't even know where my phone was—he bled a lot. Then he stopped breathing; and his blood made a spot on the concrete just like so many of his victims.

I found my phone with my purse. I considered calling you and telling you where I was, but it was dead and I couldn't even get a Wifi signal to search a map app to see where I was. It took me a while—it felt like hours—to even find my way out of the lair he'd created for his fun and games with his victims where no one would hear them scream. By the time I breathed fresh air, it was dark and cold. I wasn't certain of the time or the day of the week. I knew I'd lost a big chuck of time and I didn't know exactly how big the chunk was. Freezing rain was falling. My wet, sticky, drying pants felt horrible, I felt horrible. I felt like every joint in my body was burning. I recognized my location, although how I will not tell you. I hadn't planned to remain anonymous, but I will tell you why shortly. I managed to walk to your location, which wasn't very far away.

Or at least to the location of your office. I thought about how pissed you would be to know the killer you hunted was not far from you, hiding in plain sight. I don't know if you were there that late at night or not. I approached the desk sergeant, Sergeant Lutz, by the name on the plate in front of him. I barely got out my request to see you. He said, and I quote, "We don't take care of bag ladies here! This is not a fucking homeless shelter, and you can't spend the night in a warm, dry cell. There's a shelter about three blocks down." He pointed with his thumb like a hitchhiker down the street. "Now get the fuck out of here!" I considered saying something else and decided it probably wouldn't do much good. I was dirty and disheveled. I stank. I admit when I finally managed to get home and see myself in a mirror, I was appalled. However, at that moment, I was angry. I will never again ignore a bag lady, not that I was ever unkind to one. Bag ladies and street people are also human beings. As I walked out, I heard him remark, "Stinking bitch should learn to a do a proper cop and squat so she doesn't piss all over her pants."

I walked another hour in the cold, in the dark to where the holiday party had been the previous night. Thinking each step took me away from that horrid place was what kept me going. My stench was a blessing in disguise. No one bothered me, much less approached me. I was tired, starving, aching, and over all miserable. I had a bump on my head and a headache, probably from whenever he let me plop to the concrete floor. I wouldn't be surprised if I had a concussion, but I didn't go to a hospital. And I was thankful to be alive and walking and feeling the pain.

I found my car still where I'd left it parked for the party the night before. I drove home without incident, ignoring the sticky, nastiness of my smelly self. The heater of my car couldn't seem to penetrate the numb and cold that filled me. I felt as if I'd somehow left my body and was watching myself drive home.

At home, I peeled off my clothes and tied them into a plastic bag. I planned to never wear them again. I changed my purse and threw that into the bag, too. I want no reminders of my time with this monster. I kept the running shoes, because the laces aided in my escape. Everything else went into the trash and I made certain it went into the garbage truck days later. I showered. Then I soaked. I confess I have since had to shower several times a day, as I try to keep the nasty feeling off me and the horrid smell out of my nose. I made a blazing fire in my fireplace. I keep my nice-smelling candle warmer going all the time, too. I ate my favorite food. I plan to stay in shape in case I need to again at some time save myself. God knows no one else is going to. At the same time, I plan to enjoy everything, including my favorite foods. I plan to never again skip the cake.

This timetable as you can read is very vague. I'm doing this to make certain you can't retrace my steps or locate me. I am not writing this to clear my conscience. My conscience is clear. There is no doubt this was self-defense. Knowing what this monster was capable of, knowing what he planned to do to me, and knowing beyond a shadow of a doubt he would have done it to me had I not stopped him, keeps me moving forward. I knew it was me or him, and I chose me. I am only angry that I had to lower myself to near his evil level and become someone I never planned to be in order to save myself. If and when you ever step into that place, you'll find purses and shoes and jewelry of all those victims on a shelf like a trophy display.

I sleep well at night knowing my grandmother's ring isn't on that shelf, and no other woman ever has to experience his terror. I look forward to this season of giving and I embrace this beautiful holiday of Christmas with a renewed sense of thanksgiving that I am alive to enjoy it and share it with those whom I love instead of them having to grieve around my grave. They do not even know how close they came to being there. And although tomorrow is never promised, I know you will not be investigating my murder, not today. I thank you for all the hard work and hours of energy you put into the investigation. I'm sorry I robbed you of stopping him. But I am in no way sorry he's stopped.

Don't ask how I found your home address. You're not that hard to find, and the how is not important. I will not come talk to you. I will not tell you where his lair was. I only write this to tell you your Christmas wish has been granted. You, too, can rest easy knowing your daughters are safe from him. Merry Christmas.

Sincerely,

One of Santa's Elves

Detective Anthony Grayson stared at the letter, handwritten with blue ink on college ruled notebook filler paper.

The Christmas card in which the letter had arrived had been delivered to his home. His personal address was printed clearly on the front of the envelope. The purchased Christmas card had a photo of a polar bear wearing a Santa hat on the front. Inside in pre-printed script were the simple words *Merry Christmas.* There was no signature. There was also no return address on the envelope. There was no postmark. He didn't expect one. Letters these days went through machines. The stamp was a Christmas stamp. The envelope was closed with four Christmas stickers, and Tony bet his next paycheck the glue of the envelope had not been licked.

To tell the truth, he'd been dumbfounded that he had even received a Christmas card. Ten minutes ago, when he discovered what was an obvious holiday greeting card in his stack of junk mail, he felt elated that someone had thought enough and taken the time to send him one. Because since he and his ex-wife had split two years ago, he had received little in the way of anything but bills and junk and letters from his attorney.

Carefully, he retrieved a clear plastic bag. When he touched the card and the envelope again, he did so wearing a pair of blue nitrile gloves, and he let them drop into the plastic bag. He was obligated to turn it into the lab crew so they could check for fingerprints or any clue as to the letter's origin or the author's identify. He held little hope. If the letter writer was smart enough to escape the Red-Scarf Rapist. she was probably smart enough to remain anonymous. It was too bad, too. He would have liked to leave that cute polar bear card in the middle of his empty kitchen table. His small place of residence was void of decoration and character, including any signs of the season.

His next day was grueling. He felt as if he was interrogated regarding the note and Christmas card. Was he certain this was the first one he received? Did he recognize the handwriting? Has he been withholding evidence? He was forced to keep his clenched fists out of sight in his pockets. He gave not one, but two reports to various people regarding his stance on finding the Red Scarf Rapist and where his team stood when it came to apprehending this monster. His team had done nothing but work and study and dig and check dead-end leads and phone records since the first victim had been discovered in the park wearing only a bra and matching panties with a red wool scarf tied around her neck. She had been tortured, raped, and strangled with the scarf. From her countless signs of torture, Tony had no doubt she had been in a great deal of pain before she took her last breath. And he'd vowed to catch this monster no matter how long it took. Since then, there had been more victims, but somehow less clues. This murdering rapist knew how to stay hidden and leave not one useable lead in any direction they could follow to catch him.

And now someone had not only managed to escape him, but had stopped him for good. Tony's only regret in that idea was that he hadn't been the one to do the honors or applaud this woman. At least Tony had been smart enough to use his phone to take a photo of the letter, the card, and the envelope before handing them over to the evidence team. He remained in Captain Turrik's office after the very angry, very frustrated mayor left.

Tony understood the frustration. He'd started feeling it about a week after the first victim had been discovered, and it had only escalated since. His team of five people shared their frustration with him as well. They had tons of evidence taken from crime scenes and off dead bodies, and they had interviewed hundreds of people. But he felt no closer to actually finding a killer.

Susan Miller, the only woman assigned to his team, had a cup of coffee waiting for him when he finally managed to leave Captain Turrik's office. "Do you have any of your ass left? Or did it all get chewed off?"

Tony chuckled and thanked her for the coffee. It was a shot of Jack he craved right then, but the coffee served in a pinch. And it was always pinching since he hadn't had a drink in two years.

"Do you really think a woman managed to escape the RSR?" she asked.

He and his team had long ago shortened the name of the Red Scarf Rapist to just RSR when they spoke about him.

"I certainly hope so."

"Even if she never tells us where and who he is, I'd sure like to meet her," Susan commented. "And shake her hand."

"Me, too." Tony took a big swallow of the coffee and burned a streak down his throat to his stomach.

"When does Peterson get back?" Susan asked. "Not that I care. He doesn't do much when he's here. I just wondered when I'd have to put up with his sarcastic shit again."

"I don't know really, and I don't care," Tony lied. The truth was he did care. He'd picked his team, all colleagues with whom he'd previously worked, all good investigators, people he could depend on, and officers who noticed details. Peterson hadn't been his pick, and Tony had never been told just how Peterson managed to be assigned to the team. Peterson hadn't offered much in the way of driving the investigation forward. Then he informed Tony he had vacation that had been approved before this investigation started, and he had plane tickets and cruise ship tickets and he was going somewhere warm for a week. It wasn't long before Tony discovered Peterson went somewhere warm often. He preferred to work several twelve-hour shifts in a row so he could have several days off in a row. They were not far into this investigation when Tony decided to just let him go and do his thing.

"I feel the same way, he's a such a pain in the ass. I was surprised to see they didn't make him cancel his vacation, though, in the midst of all these victims."

"That's not up to me," Tony commented, keeping his feelings to himself. The truth was, he'd wondered that himself. As soon as this was over, Tony planned to report Peterson's lack of help to the captain and request he never have to work with Peterson again.

"What's on the agenda today?" she asked.

"I plan to look at cold cases of missing women, see if anything ties into any of our cases. Our mystery writer said there were others."

"Sounds like as good a direction to go as any. It's certainly better than being stalled. Maybe when RSR first started, he left more clues, something someone missed."

He had to agree as he sat down with his cup of coffee.

"Too bad we can't tell the public, not without having evidence and a body."

He had thought about letting it slip during the press conference and try to cover himself with an, "Oops, sorry." Because he knew as well as anyone, it was easier to ask forgiveness than it was to ask permission. But fuses were already short, and the last thing he ever wanted to do was anything that would make this case worse. "True," Tony agreed. "Let's start digging and find some certainty and proof."

"Then we can move on to finding the next killer," Susan commented.

"Yes, indeed."

"I also brought donuts," Susan said, pointed them out on a nearby table.

"Even better."

It was well after dark when Captain Turrik ordered him to go home and get some sleep. He didn't. He went to an AA meeting. It wasn't his usual, but he knew he'd better go. Jack was really calling his name today. The meeting helped.

When he finally arrived back at his small house, he found an envelope inside his front door. This one had no stamp, no address, just his name. Someone had slipped it through the mail slot on his front door.

Dear Detective Grayson,

When you called a press conference, I expected you to share with the public the Red Scarf Rapist is dead and that the women of our wonderful city are safe, at least from him. The last thing I expected was for you to state there was a person of interest and you asked that person to come forward and share information.

If you are referring to me, I already told you, I'm not coming forward. You can thank Sergeant Lutz for that. On more than one occasion, I worked to do the right thing. Number one, I took a cab instead of driving when I thought it wasn't safe for me to drive. I will never again do that. Number two, I tried, asked, requested, to speak to you and was turned away rudely. I'm not even certain I could again find that murderer's building. It was dark, I was dazed, and at first, all I concentrated on was putting distance between it and me.

Tony paused in his reading and thought that was a lie. He knew sheer terror did one of two things—it either sharpened one's focus or it caused amnesia. Either way, the eyes still saw things that registered in the brain. Tony was certain if he could get his elf into his car and drive her around, landmarks would be familiar. He read on.

As I drove home, I regretted not staying in your station and telling you or at least telling someone. I regret, still, seeing lingering fear in the face of the public. But I'm sure there would be, some lowlife lawyer, somewhere, claiming I should have done something different. There would perhaps be someone, also, who claimed he deserved rehabilitation or he might even have gotten off for some stupid reason or better yet, a plea bargain, or an insanity plea. In cases like this the victim has virtually no rights and the criminal has every right. The victim gets protesters in front of her house. The criminal gets a free meal and free therapy.

I did not—could not—chance that. I also couldn't chance the idea he might get the better of me a second time if I hesitated in any way.

I am certain that if he made it all the way to the lethal injection, which you and I both know he rightly deserved, there would still be protestors at his execution. There would forever be someone who argued he had rights and deserved life, no matter what he stole from his victims or planned to steal from me, a plan which he didn't keep a secret from me. But then, for reasons I can't tell you at this time, I doubt he'd make it even to prison, or the county jail.

So, for now, I remain anonymous. But you haven't even said thank you that your Christmas wish has been granted. Nor have you told the public the Red Scarf Rapist has been stopped. But then, I guess in order to do that, you'd need to find him and verify everything I've told you. I'll think on that. In the meantime, I am going to hug my family close today. I suggest you do the same. Get some rest, you look tired. You should put up a Christmas tree, too, it'll bring some light and Christmas joy into your life.

Sincerely,

Santa's Elf

Tony carefully placed the second handwritten letter in a clear plastic bag before he headed back out into the night to give it to the lab guys. And he wondered again just how this woman could know his address. He had never felt the need for cameras. His house was small, older, and could be, if he did any shopping or decorating, comfortable.

The neighborhood was mostly people who had lived in it for the past forty or so years. Tomorrow, in the daylight, he'd check and see if anyone saw anything or anyone had cameras that might have picked up a clue. Now, he was too exhausted. His head ached. His empty stomach grumbled. By the time he got back to his house again, he fell fully clothed onto his bed and slept until after sunrise.

In an effort to wake up and feel human, he stood in the shower until the hot water ran out. He drove twenty-one miles out of the way to his home town of Mossy Point where he stepped into *Signorino's Bakery and Brew*. Lizzy Signorino made the best cinnamon twists and coffee just the way he liked it. Tony was greeted by Lizzy's twin brother.

"Hey, Tony number two. How's life in the big city?"

Tony Grayson chuckled. "Hey, Tony number one. Do you think we'll ever escape the football team nicknames?"

Antonio Signorino grinned and shrugged. "Why should we? Our high school football careers may be over and the coach who gave us those numbers for names may be up at the senior center, but you're still Tony and I'm still Tony. I suppose we could let it go if you're tired of being number two."

Tony took a bite of his cinnamon roll and washed it down with a sip of his coffee. "Not really. I think I'd like to hold on to those good times for as long as possible, if that's okay with you." For the first time in months after the first Red Scarf Rapist killing, Tony allowed himself to relax as he and his high school football teammate caught up. It was nice to leave the murder case all behind him and think about something else, even if it was only for a little while. The fact that the streets were lined with Christmas lights and the coffee shop looked a little like something out of a Christmas movie made his heart a bit lighter and renewed his idea there was something good in the world where killers lurked and hid and tortured women.

An hour later, he headed into the precinct, feeling rejuvenated after smelling the yeasty air and letting Lizzy's coffee and Tony number one's conversation warm him. For the first time in a very long time, his head was clearer and he didn't crave a drink. But he was late, and his usual parking spot was taken. So were all the others within a block of the station door. He was forced to park several blocks away and race through the cold, but that was fine. Like the coffee and the comforting feeling of home, the brisk air filled him with a renewed sense of purpose. He was determined to have answers, no matter how small, by the end of today.

He didn't.

As he trudged through the dark and bitter cold back to his car after another frustrating day where he see-sawed back and forth about telling the public or not telling the public, he couldn't help but curse the way the day had deflated his sense of determination. His eyes burned from reading files. The discussion held by his team was just a stuck record, playing the same song from all the previous discussions. His gut felt like a Tasmanian devil swirled through it with the idea his secret pen pal would have posed in photos like the other victims if she hadn't escaped.

All in all, he thought the case had become some sort of monster with big, pointed teeth who was chewing away at him bit by bit.

Maybe he should pass this entire case off to someone else. It wouldn't be too hard. There were so many others chomping at the bit to have a look at it, anyway. And all day, after his visit to Mossy Point earlier, he questioned his reasons for holding on to it and staying in the city.

Because he was no quitter, that's why. Every photo he looked at today added an ounce of determination. He would end this. He had to.

Tony had moved here when he married. But that was over now. So even if he was determined to solve this case there was still the question of why stay? Especially when the entire time he'd been breathing his home town air, he hadn't longed for a single drink. He decided then he'd give himself a week. Even if the case wasn't solved, and he had no body to show the world the Red Scarf Rapist was fucking dead, he'd still move back to Mossy Point. He could commute into the city every day. Others did.

Right now, though, he considered another AA meeting. This case could take away all he'd built in the way of a sober life for the past two years if he let it and remained in the city.

He changed his mind about the meeting when he saw there was a letter stuck under the windshield wiper of his car when he finally made his way back to it. He climbed into his car before he opened it and read it. He decided then that he wasn't going to waste the time or the resources taking it to the lab guys. The letters thus far offered nothing more than the words written on them.

Dear Detective Grayson,

I understand Sergeant Lutz harassed and questioned some poor woman he thought might be me. Shame on him. He should be fired. But then I thought he should be fired after the way he talked to me. Yet, he's still there. Still treating people like shit. Did he take the oath to protect and serve like the rest of you did? Just wondering. What exactly is his job description?

All my best,

Santa's Elf

He had heard about Lutz questioning a woman when he'd arrived late. He'd spent the morning studying every crime photo, looking for something new. His letter writer had to be someone close in order to know about Lutz since that incident had happened shortly after Lutz came on duty at six a.m. Deciding his pen pal was right and he shouldn't share further letters, he tucked the letter into his pocket.

"Who are you?" he asked out loud in the silence of his car. He discovered he didn't need his AA meeting after all. He grabbed a sandwich and went home. In his small living room, there was only his television on a small stand, a recliner, and his laptop on a TV tray. He didn't get visitors. Gone were the days where he invited his colleagues over for Sunday games or poker nights with lots of beer and snacks. It had been drunk fests like those that ruined his marriage and put him into a hole that had been almost impossible to crawl out of.

Yes, his life these days was lonely, but it was clean and clear. And he didn't mind being alone. But now, he watched the news, watched his press conferences with new eyes. He watched the crowd, looking for a woman who might be writing him letters as he longed to put a face to his mystery pen pal. He didn't spot anyone he thought could be his elf. But he woke with a new sense of direction.

The next morning, he was up much earlier. Again, he went out of his way to Lizzy's coffee shop. He was testing the waters, so to speak, seeing how the morning commute was into city during rush hour. And he made sure he allowed himself the time and vowed he wouldn't be late. He treated himself to pie as he sat at the counter and again enjoyed the feeling of being home. No one asked him about the case. There was no TV to bring anyone bad news. There was only Lizzy putting up more Christmas decorations. There was soft classical Christmas music playing from overhead speakers. There were familiar faces, people slapping him on the shoulder telling him they were glad to see him. The words, "Merry Christmas" echoed about the place. The entire atmosphere did leave him feeling merry. And lighter. And better.

It was that sense of home that carried him through the day, even though he spent it reading more files and studying every aspect of the case like a college student cramming for a final and failing anyway. When he arrived home, he found yet more mail just inside his front door. This time there was a small bubble envelope. Finding himself as eager to get a message as he was to discover the identity of the letter writer, he ripped open the envelope like a kid opening a Christmas gift. As it turned out, it was a Christmas gift.

Dear Detective Grayson,

I watched your press conference. You look tired. Why are you not resting easy now that the Red Scarf Rapist has been stopped? Why are you wearing the same tie two days in a row? Please accept the enclosed

Christmas gift—a new tie which I feel will look great with either a green or blue shirt, or your usual white. Merry Christmas early!

Your Elf

The signature had changed from Santa's Elf to Your Elf. He did feel as if these personal notes were like love letters from his own personal elf. It had now been four full days after the delivery of his first letter. Tack on a few days of mail delivery, and that made it almost a full week. If the Red Scarf Rapist was really lying dead in a pool of his own blood, he was bound to be pretty ripe and stink by now. "Please tell me where he is," he said out loud in his empty house.

He, of course, got no reply.

The next day, Susan, said, "I'm taking a break from all this morbid shit and giving my brain a rest. I feel like my eyes are beginning to blur looking at crime scene photos." She spent the next two hours putting up a three-foot Christmas tree in the corner of the room. Tony didn't argue it. He could tell everyone on his team was becoming as burned out as he felt. They were just as tired of looking at death pictures and reading reports and finding no new needle in the bloody haystack.

Ten minutes later, Johnny, the mail guy came around. "Hey! Grayson! You got a letter!"

The single envelope Johnny held sent his heart pounding. He couldn't understand why he'd get one here, now, when others had been delivered to his car and his house. Everyone gathered around. He carefully opened it, knowing he couldn't hide this one or keep it to himself, that it would have to be reported and handed over to the lab guys. Inside the envelope was a single yellow small piece of paper with adhesive on the back. It stuck to the envelope and took extra effort getting it out.

Dear Detective Grayson,

This elf wants to know: Who the fuck leaked my letter to press?

This note was not signed as Santa's elf or Your elf.

Tony hadn't known someone had leaked the letter. He looked at the envelope. Again, there was no postmark, and he wondered if his elf was somehow able to get a letter into the delivered mail. He supposed anything was possible. He muttered a profanity under his breath before he assigned another team member, Harry Hilton, to find out who leaked the information. Neither he nor his team members had time for this bullshit. Yet, he found his time consumed with damage control instead of following through with search warrants for more phone records as he planned. They had a killer to catch or a dead body to find. He spent the next two hours reading the news media and watching news on the TV kept in that meeting room for that very reason. He bit his tongue and kept his hands in his pockets to keep his rage hidden as he saw parts of the first letter he'd received and dealt with the backlash.

The press had a field day.

The mayor had something that resembled a seizure.

The captain had a question/answer session that was mostly questions with no answers. Still in the end, no one fessed up to leaking the letter.

There was a number of people who knew about the letters, even the mayor and probably his secretary had been informed. Tony could spend his time fighting the system or he could roll with it. He chose to roll with it. And when Harry Hilton discovered Lutz had been in the evidence lab a half hour before his shift began, Tony advised Harry to report it to the captain. Tony managed to relax a bit after he took a lunch break and spent some time on a video call with his girls. They always grounded him and reminded him why he was working so hard to make the world a safer place. They told him all about what they asked Santa to bring them, and Tony was very thankful for mail order.

When he got home, there was a letter in his house.

He could easily install a camera, see who delivered these messages. But just then, he was more eager for the actual letters and the information contained in them than he was knowing the identity of the author. Besides he didn't allow himself the time.

Dear Detective Grayson,

I ask that you do not share my words. You are not going to find me by checking for fingerprints on the paper or studying the loops of my G's. So just read my story and listen, learn, and perhaps put this all to rest in the right way. Thank you. Why are you wasting your time with yet another press conference to URGE the person of interest (me) to come forward regarding the case of the Red Scarf Rapist. Forget it, Tony. And if it's your head honcho making demands, tell him I said to forget it. Can I call you Tony? I do feel like we've reached a level of friendship where we can be on a first-name basis. Not that we're really friends. Friends have cake and coffee together and chat about non-important things. I don't plan to have coffee with you, at least not now, but who knows what the future will bring. And what I'm chatting about is very important. For now, the answer is no, I'm not coming forward. To tell you the truth, Tony, if you had pursued the Red Scarf Rapist as much as you are pursuing the person of interest, we probably wouldn't be corresponding as we are. And I am telling you the truth here. Besides, I guess you've reached a dead end in your investigation. The Red Scarf Rapist is not going to be leaving you any new clues.

Someone there, hopefully not you because I trust you, and want to trust you, shared my first letter to you or at least bits and pieces of it with the press. If I had to guess, it was probably Lutz. He's the only one who seems to have extra time on his hands. And golly, gee whiz, the entire city is now on a scavenger hunt to find the Red Scarf Rapist's dead body and to find the person who killed him. A few of them are protesting that I should be arrested. My goal here was not to be on the news, not to be dissected in the media, not to be blamed for defending myself. And someone there has turned this into a circus. I certainly hope it wasn't you, Tony. If it was, your tactic won't draw me out of the woodwork. If the circus and the leaks continue, I'll blame you because that little note today will be the only one sent to the police station. My sharing of all of this was so you could end it. I could have kept it all to myself, confessed it only to my Priest, and let the Red Scarf Rapist rot in the sound-proof torture chamber he, himself, created. But I didn't do that. Please don't make me sorry I went this route. I'm off to a family gift exchange. I'm encouraging you to do the same—enjoy your family, spend time with loved ones especially those beautiful little girls of yours. You never know when you might be kidnapped, tortured, and/or murdered. As I found out the hard way, it can happen any moment of any day.

By the way, I was right. The tie looks great on you. Here, accept this one, too. You should wear something other than white. Be adventurous. Wear something daring like red or purple. Live it up. The Red Scarf Rapist showed us all how short life can be. Don't you agree? Play some Christmas music. Enjoy the season. Will you be getting together with your colleagues for a party? You should start the tradition.

Your Elf

There was a large envelope inside his front door when he woke the next morning. It held a letter and the latest edition of a tabloid.

There was no salutation, no Dear Tony, just:

OMG, Tony, The National Secret News tabloid apparently has photos of the inside of the Red Scarf Rapist's lair. Strange, the place looks nothing like what I saw, what I remember, or what haunts my nightmares. I wonder where they got those. Surely, they would never make those details up. I still wonder even more where they got excerpts of my first letter to you. Anyone in your precinct had a sudden bonus or bank deposit more than the usual meager paycheck lately? Lutz, maybe? Reading in between the lines of the article, I feel they insinuated that I might be the Red Scarf Rapist's partner or girlfriend who helped him kidnap women but then got tired of it or scared or jealous and murdered him. Because they find it hard to believe a victim could have escaped him, so now they are reporting that the Red Scarf Rapist was 'murdered' by an intended victim or an accomplice. They have a fuzzed-out photo of the back of a woman they claim to be the intended victim and letter writer. And I'll be honest, it looks nothing like me even though I don't look at the back of myself very often. I don't have brown hair. And if this is another tactic to get me to say what I do look like so you can find me, forget it. Like the police leaving out important details of a crime in order to know that they have the right suspect, I left out pertinent details about my experience with the Red Scarf Rapist. Now I hope I really can trust you and you aren't sharing my words, because I have so much more to tell you.

You should probably sit down for this.

That prick deserved to be tortured as he'd tortured his victims. He deserved to live as long as possible in as much pain as possible, just as he had done to his victims. I really considered stringing him up by his heels above the biggest dried blood spot in the place and give him a taste of his own medicine. But I knew I didn't have time for that. And the last thing I wanted to do was lower myself to be exactly like him. He did, however, manage to answer some questions and provide some information that might give families closure. Here's some names you might check out: Clare Watson, Garman Everson, and Valerie Moore. And check out a field at a farm on Galston Road in a little town called Williamstown. I would take cadaver dogs and whatever lab people with chemicals to test the soil or radar or whatever you use to search for bodies. There must be a red barn there, and I would advise you to search behind it. But before you do that and before you share this information with anyone, especially your captain or the mayor or anyone else who might be in contact with higher ups, check out who owns that property.

And here's more you should know. It's about another detective in your precinct on your team, Detective Billy Peterson. He's on vacation, isn't he? Or he hasn't shown up for work, has he? I would have told you about him sooner, but I had to do some research before I blurted out that information. You see, there was nothing like newspaper clippings or news photos in that torture chamber, nothing to show the Red Scarf Rapist may have been following your investigation or checking how close you and your team—or anyone else—might be to catching him.

I got the impression he didn't need to know because he already knew the status of the investigation.

There were, however, other photos, in frames, photos that looked like family photos one would see in a home. There was a photo in that little kitchen where the Red Scarf Rapist made his sandwich. It was a photo of a family standing in front of a Christmas tree. I'm pretty sure it was the same photo sent out as Christmas cards by a certain national representative. I'm sure you are well aware of who Detective Peterson's mother is. And I'm sure if you don't do this right, there will be a ten-alarm fire at the building that holds his little torture chamber. All evidence will be destroyed. And I would have a new target painted on my back. While I doubt anyone could or would find me, I can't take that chance. As I investigated Detective Peterson, after learning the identity of the Red Scarf Rapist, I found a lot more than meets the eye and a lot more than the Red Scarf Rapist, so you should check him out under the radar, like I did. I'm trusting you here, Tony, to do the right thing the right way. I know you want to get to the bottom of this and put the Red Scarf Rapist to bed forever, but if you go charging in without dotting all the I's and crossing all the T's and minding your P's and Q's, you're going to have a backwash of misery, and Detective Peterson will be made a victim. I also know if I had just told you earlier the other details about my abduction and my escape and who the Red Scarf Rapist was, there would be people involved who couldn't be trusted, people who would work and do whatever is necessary to cover up his crimes. Do the right thing, with the right people. And go slowly. I don't want to see anything happen to you.

Your Elf

Tony swore out loud and considered calling in sick. He sure felt like he might puke. And he hadn't even eaten anything yet.

Good evening, Tony,

So, this evening you were at the Twisted Lime, drinking virgin Shirley Temples. Good for you. I'm glad to see this case has not pushed you off the wagon you worked so hard to climb up on in the last two years. Yes, I know about your drinking problem. I know about your divorce. Don't ask me how I know. And no, I am not stalking you. Although I think you may be unconsciously stalking me since you walked in to where I was. What are the odds? Maybe we should both buy a lottery ticket. You sat at the bar and nursed one pink drink after another. I'm glad you got your shit together. You've got two little girls who need you even if you aren't sharing a residence with them. You are surprised I would know so much about you? It is the only one positive thing about Sergeant Lutz treating me like shit. It allowed me a few hours to check you out and make sure you were on the up and up before I contacted you and shared all my information.

Were you just celebrating the season, or were you conflicted over everything I shared with you to this moment? Worse yet, did you already investigate your colleague, Detective Peterson, perhaps go to his house, and find it empty? Did you dig further and discover maybe he had something to do with a teenager—a girl, I might add—that went missing when he was in high school? He was questioned, but nothing came of it. Nothing came of him being questioned regarding a grade school boy who fell off a roof, either, despite the questionable circumstances. Don't ask me how I learned of these incidents. If there's one thing I know how to do, it's investigate, it's knowing when and how and where to dig for clues. While I understand these things happened to Peterson as a juvenile, I also understand every profession, teachers, doctors, nurses, even playground monitors these days, all require a background check. What is required for entering the police academy? How does one get promoted to detective? How does one get beyond a background check when there are suspicious happenings in one's background? Did you check the names I gave to you and did the times they went missing coincide with Peterson being on vacation or out sick or even once at an investigative workshop? Did you notice one of the young women missing disappeared at college while Detective Peterson was there giving a seminar? Did you also see that with being the child of a prominent congressman—or in this case, congresswoman—how many things have been expunged and swept under a rug or hidden away like a skeleton in a closet on Halloween? Amazing. I also see where he was caught shoplifting more than once. And he was placed on probation in college for plagiarism. To add insult to that injury, he somehow has a degree behind his name. Yet, his transcript seems a bit short on the number of required hours. Again, I am amazed. Please, Tony tread carefully. By the looks of his record, he had, and still has, a very powerful family covering his tracks and paving the way for him and cleaning up his messes. It probably won't matter that he's dead in a place where he murdered so many people. Innocent people have disappeared for less, and I'm terrified to think the lengths that may be taken to protect his reputation, as well as his family's reputation, now. Frightening. I was terrified just thinking about it, even beyond the sheer terror of being at the hands of the Red Scarf Rapist. Now, I am afraid for you. I know you want to do the right thing. I saw the struggle on your face this evening as you nursed your Shirley Temples. I'm afraid, also, that you might be surrounded by people who will stop at nothing to help this family keep their secrets safe. I'm sorry you had to find out this way. Please be careful.

Your Elf

Two days later, Tony sat at the counter of *Signorino's Bakery and Brew*. In the area off to his right, several people from the local grocery store were enjoying their annual Christmas party. He took a deep breath and then a sip of the richest coffee he'd ever tasted. Oddly, he felt lighter than he had in the past twelve years. Yes, reaching the rank of detective had taken a lot of work. Yet, he hadn't known or recognized the weight of it on his shoulders until it was gone.

Antonio Signorino, Tony number one, came near and topped his cup off. "I saw you on the news this morning. So, you caught the Red Scarf Rapist?"

"That's right." Tony number two didn't elaborate.

"Well, way to go. You're a hero," Antonio said.

Tony didn't feel like a hero. In fact, he felt like the biggest liar on the face of the earth. That feeling came with a large degree of numbness.

Underneath the delicious taste of his coffee was a lingering feeling of nausea he fought to ignore.

"I had a lot of help," he muttered.

His instructions when it came to the Red Scarf Rapist were: Just stick to the facts. And the facts were, the Red Scarf Rapist was dead. He'd been killed when he refused to surrender and fired shots at the police who were attempting to apprehend him. Unfortunately, Detective Billy Peterson had been injured by the gunfire and died on the scene, also.

Tony had been told to read exactly those words during the press conference, and he had, thinking he might vomit at any moment. He figured he would be on his deathbed and still remember the sight of Billy Peterson's bloated body. He also knew he'd never forget the sight of all the torture equipment. Peterson's computer had a log of every victim. And as he'd been told by his secret elf, there were purses and shoes and jewelry, as well as classroom books and backpacks belonging to all his victims.

After the press conference, Detective Tony Grayson was placed on indefinite leave for firing his service weapon, even though he'd never even taken his weapon from its secured holster. The fact about that part was, he was on leave until it was decided what do to about him because he didn't follow protocol. He didn't report to his captain his suspicions about his colleague or what he discovered when he began to connect the dots from property in Williamstown to a warehouse down the street from the precinct. When he'd gotten a judge friend to sign a search warrant for the warehouse without divulging any information to his captain or the mayor who could have—and probably would have contacted Congresswoman Peterson—and he'd stepped into the warehouse with only his team and investigators from the state police, he had angered a lot of people. He heard Peterson's mother had even showed up in Turrik's office, but he hadn't been there to witness that.

By then, the investigation was already in motion. And she hadn't been able to stop it.

Before placing him on leave, Captain Turrik had looked Tony in the eye and told him he had to be able to trust his officers and detectives.

Tony had held the captain's gaze and replied, "You trusted me to find a killer, and I did. I just really hope no one leaks to the press who the real rapist was."

He didn't get a box and clean out his desk, but he took home things he couldn't live without if he didn't return. He hadn't been asked to turn in his badge or his gun. But trust went both ways, and they all knew it. He knew deep in his heart if he had done things any differently, the public would still think the Red Scarf Rapist was out there ready to snatch another woman. With the information Peterson had in his computer, Tony had been able to give closure to several other families of missing women. He didn't like that the world didn't get to see the monster Peterson really was, but he was satisfied with everything else.

"So, what's the plan, Tony number two?" Antonio asked.

"I'm not sure yet. But I have the feeling I'll soon be looking for a quieter place, here probably."

Antonio placed a large piece of cake in front of him.

"I didn't order that."

"Nope. It's courtesy of the woman at the end of the counter."

Tony looked down and saw her. She wasn't anyone he recognized. She was pretty, with strawberry blond hair and vibrant green eyes. She was noticeable and was the kind of woman he knew Peterson would have made some comment about. She offered him a small smile before she held her coffee mug up and offered him a salute.

Then she winked.

For a long moment Tony stared at her. Could she escape the Red Scarf Rapist, a man he now knew had police training? She wrote in her letter she was often underestimated. He saw where she could be given her petite size. Thoughts swirled through his mind. His heart raced in his chest. With every ounce of his being, he was eternally grateful he was seeing her living and breathing. He was not forced to study her dead corpse or photos of her crime scene. There would be no inch-thick file with her name on it. At least not right now.

He picked up the plate with the cake and his mug of coffee, having every intention of moving closer to her, his breath catching with idea he would finally learn the name of his elf.

Someone stopped him by slapping him on the back of his shoulder. "Nice to see you back in town." It was Chief of Police James 'Mac' McLane.

Tony sat back down on his stool and set his mug and plate down, too. "Nice to see you, too, Mac."

"Isn't that just the best cake?"

Tony took a bite. Rich flavor of almond and butter melted in his mouth. "It's delicious, like heaven on a fork."

"It's something called Italian Christmas cake. Lizzy got the recipe from her grandma."

"Do you want a piece?" Tony offered.

"No," Mac refused. "I've already had two. If I'm not careful, Lizzy's baking will make me fat."

"I doubt that," Tony said with a chuckle. He glanced down the counter. The redhead was still there, also enjoying a slice of cake. Tony was a seasoned cop, trained to see details, and he couldn't miss the healing abrasion on her wrist as she lifted the fork to her mouth to take a bite of cake. "Besides, do you know what life taught me just this week?"

"What?" Mac asked.

"That we should all enjoy something rich and delicious every day, that we should enjoy the cake if we want it."

"Yeah, I heard about your case, but you solved it, you stopped that raping murderer. I'm sorry to hear about your colleague who was killed in the crossfire."

Unable to lie further, Tony said nothing.

"I know we were supposed to meet at ten today, but when I saw you in here, I thought we could just have an impromptu meeting now," Mac suggested. "Unless you need to talk about something personal."

"No, this is fine. I considered asking you about a job."

"You don't plan to stay in the city?"

"I'm on leave now, but I don't plan to go back. That case took the wind out of my sails. And well, city life has never been for me. I thought I'd come back to something more familiar. I'm even looking at buying the old mill building property."

"Really?"

"Yes, I think I'll buy it. I have a meeting with the realtor this afternoon. I think taking my time and fixing it up would be therapeutic for me."

"Are you sure you want to do that? I mean have you ever wondered just how many teenagers have snuck into that vacant place and lost their virginity? I would imagine every room has been christened."

"I promise I won't move in until I pay someone to clean it thoroughly."

They both chuckled.

"Although," Tony continued, "I do plan to put up a Christmas tree there, and add some Christmas cheer to my life. I didn't seem to have the desire to do that at my place in the city."

"Well, I'm sure we can find a place for you here, but you take your time. Allow yourself to heal and decide. It wasn't that long ago that I was in the same place as you."

The way Mac spoke those words left Tony thinking he knew more about the Red Scarf Rapist case than what the news reported about the rapist being shot and an officer also being killed. That idea was confirmed when Mac asked, "I understand there might be a state representative involved. How will this affect her?"

Tony shrugged. "I'm no longer involved, but all the right people are—and it's a lot of the right people. They're questioning her on how much she knew and how much she might have even helped. They'll study everything from phone records to property sales. I heard other bodies have been found on property owned by..." he paused, thinking he already said too much, then thought what the hell. "The family," he finished. "She won't be able to sweep any of this under a rug and go on as if nothing happened." While he was confident the right people were handling it, the idea he worked so closely with a killer was like a coiled snake in his gut.

"I see. Nice tie," Mac complimented. It was a polite way to change the subject. Mac was a smart cop with FBI experience under his belt. He was bound to understand the position in which Tony had been placed with the Red Scarf Rapist case.

"Thank you. It was a Christmas gift."

"Well, someone has good taste, but when and/or if you come work for me, I won't force you to wear one. Although you can if you want."

"Thank you," Tony said again. He pressed the last of his cake crumbs to his fork, working to get every bite.

Mac shook his hand as he said, "Give yourself some time, get settled, then come talk to me and we'll work out the details."

"I will, thanks."

Mac left the stool, and Tony noticed the mystery woman was no longer there. There was just an empty plate, used fork, and empty coffee mug with pretty, deep red lipstick on it looking as if she gave it half a kiss.

He jumped off his stool and raced to the end of the counter. He looked around but didn't see her anywhere. "Tony number one, did you see where the redhead who bought my cake went?"

Antonio came closer and stepped once again behind the counter. "Nope, sorry, I sure didn't. I was busy over there cleaning up a spill." He picked up the napkin sitting next to the empty plate. "It looks like she left you a note though."

"How do you know it's for me."

"Because I'm not wearing a tie," said Antonio. "And she bought your cake."

Written on the napkin in clear, blue, familiar handwriting was: *Dear Tony, the tie looks nice on you. I hope you enjoyed your cake. Thank you for everything you do and did for me. Maybe next time, we can have cake and coffee and chat like real friends. Merry Christmas.*

It was signed: *Your Elf*

"You have an elf, huh?" Antonio asked.

"I guess I do," Tony admitted.

"Aren't you the lucky one?"

"You have no idea," Tony said. He headed for the door.

"Where are you off to?" Antonio asked.

"I'm headed to watch my girls open their gifts."

"Sounds perfect."

Tony smiled. "Yes, it does. Merry Christmas, Tony number one."

"Merry Christmas, Tony number two."

The bells that jingled over the door with his exit sounded like sleigh bells.

Small Town Nightmare

The Nick and Cranny Book Store was everything Sara heard it was—coffee, pastries, comfortable chairs, and, of course, books. In no time, she found the latest true crime story from her favorite hot author, Simon Dare.

As she stood at the check-out counter, she couldn't help but notice the headline on the latest news magazine. Police Baffled by Rash of Deaths as Number Climbs.

Sara knew the story. Ten young, single women, all living alone, had been discovered dead in their beds. They appeared to have had a heart attack, despite their excellent health. There had been no signs of foul play, no sign of a second person in their bedrooms, or even in their homes.

"A book room is free with your purchase." The man behind the counter who'd just scanned the book she planned to buy grabbed Sara's attention.

"A book room?" she asked.

"Yes, it's a little, miniature room like a single, narrow room of a doll house you place between your books on your bookshelf. Some even have lights. Pick out your dream room, like where you'd like to read your book." He indicated the nearby display with several box-like miniature rooms.

Sara eyed them, each made to scale with miniature furniture.

"I'm Nick, by the way," he said. "I'm the owner."

"Sara," she replied absently as she studied the display. "These are so fun."

He nodded enthusiastically. "Yes, they are, and it's free."

Sara chose a pretty little box room with a miniature cozy chair near a fireplace. The back end of the box behind the red chair had a large half-oval window. When she flipped the switch, tiny lights lit up behind the window. They looked like stars. A yellow glow poured from the fireplace. The smaller-to-scale flooring looked like sand. "This would be the perfect room where I could read my new book," she said, "if I was three inches tall."

Nick rang up her sale, and Sara paid with her card.

"Hey, would you like to have coffee or a drink with me some time?" he asked.

"Sure. Maybe," she replied as absently as she'd told him her name. She was too busy studying her little perfect dream room, deciding where on her bookshelf she planned to place it.

She felt the touch of his hand on hers. The simple touch stopped her.

It was as if he somehow sent an electric shock up her arm. Instinctively, she pulled her hand away and met his gaze. He stared at her for a full three seconds, and Sara didn't look away. If she didn't know better, she'd think he found a way to reach into her soul with that touch.

She picked up her bag, still staring at him, wondering what he'd done to her. What should have been a simple touch to the hand felt way more invasive. A shiver crawled up her back.

"Don't forget your book," he said. He gave her a small, knowing smile.

He knew he'd unnerved her.

And she couldn't stop the creepy feeling he liked that he'd done that to her.

Creep.

She forced an equally slight smile and left with packages in hand.

Outside she ducked against the cold, spring, evening rain, yet couldn't manage to keep it from seeping down the back of her neck. Even after she reached the warmth of her car, started it, and turned on the blowing heat, she still couldn't shake the cold that filled her. Nick seemed like a genuinely nice guy, and she hadn't even been put off by his offer to have coffee. It was his touch that somehow filled her with a cold, dead feeling.

She held her hand up, studying it as she flexed her fingers and made a fist several times. She was able to move her hand at will. She touched it with her other fingers, surprised to find her skin warm.

Because her hand didn't feel warm.

"I just need to get home, out of the rain, and have some warm soup or something."

Her spoken words were loud, mixing in with the blow of the heater, and did little to convince her. The icy feeling remained all the way to her little house.

At home, she made some soup for supper, and steeped her favorite Earl Gray tea in her mother's teapot. The teapot had a hand-painted delicate red rose on both sides. Supposedly, the teapot, and one matching tea cup Sara also had, had been originally made in China and traveled across Asia, being handed down from mother to daughter for generations. The delicate pieces had crossed the Atlantic smuggled in a bag on a lifeboat of the Titanic by Sara's great-great grandmother. Sara wasn't certain she believed all the stories, but the rose was lovely, and knowing her mother had for years enjoyed tea from this pot and in the matching cup brought Sara joy as she now enjoyed her own tea.

She had several weeks of her historic, unsolved crimes podcast recorded, edited, and ready to broadcast, so she could enjoy a few evenings reading. It would open her mind to researching the next few weeks before she wrote and recorded more episodes.

She smiled as she poured tea into the matching teacup, thinking of the few things she got that belonged to her mother before her dad decided to rush in and marry the bimbo with whom he now shared space. That dumb, gold-digging bitch had cleaned out her mother's stuff so fast, Sara had almost missed getting the few treasures she had—the teapots, china sets, paintings, and some of her mother's treasured autographed books.

Sara placed her miniature room on the bookshelf between two Simon Dare books, pulled the small cord over one of the nearby books and flipped the switch. The little room lit up. The fireplace glowed, and stars sparkled through the tiny window.

"Perfect."

Warmth filled her with the rich taste of her tea as she took a swallow and loved how inviting the miniature room appeared. And her smile grew as she thought about her last conversation with her dad.

He was a lonely widower, and he understood his new wife, Lydia's, thought process. He enjoyed spending time with Lydia, said she made him feel young again, and he understood the fact the only way she'd stay with him was if he married her. Little did Lydia know, before he said 'I do,' he'd put everything, including the house Lydia just cleaned out, into a trust with only Sara's name on it. That surprise would be revealed to Lydia if, or when, something happened to her father. For now, she planned to drink tea and think of her mother every day.

Supper and tea finally warmed her soul, and later, she snuggled on her comfy sofa, covered with a green plaid throw as the rain picked up and beat against the windows.

She was well into Chapter Five when she fell asleep.

She awoke in the miniature room on her shelf.

The room smelled of new construction—wood, paint, and even a hint of plaster.

Sara looked out the window. The lights of stars were there twinkling, but there was also rain pelting against the glass. The glow of the fireplace came from true flames which added warmth to the room.

"Wow, what a dream."

Her spoken words had a slight echo. The chair, she discovered when she ran her palm across the back, was red velvet, soft and plush. There was an ottoman to match. She didn't remember there being an ottoman in her dream room when she'd bought it.

She turned slowly, taking in the entire room studying the chandelier overhead, the three-tier candelabra with tall tapers on the mantle, and the fireplace accessories of brush, shovel, poker, and tongs, all of which she didn't recall being there when she was given the little box.

Where there should be a far wall, there was no wall at all. Sara's knees grew weak seeing it, and she sank into the ottoman and stared.

What she saw was her own living room, as if she'd managed to shrink herself. Her comfy couch was huge. She was no longer on it and neither were her blanket nor her book.

She sucked in a loud breath, finding she'd somehow forgotten to breathe. She didn't think this was possible, even in a dream. She placed her hand on the velvet chair, intending to use it to give herself leverage to stand. She found her palm resting on her green, plaid throw—the same one she'd used to cover herself on the sofa. As she stared at it, dumbfounded, her attention was drawn to the nearby end table just inches from the arm of the chair. It was an end table she also didn't remember being there previously.

The pretty china cup with the familiar, hand-painted flower sat on the table.

Sara stretched forward and peered into it. It was half filled with tea, and the aroma of Earl Gray touched her senses. For the life of her, Sara couldn't remember ever being able to *smell* something in a dream.

Feeling as if she moved through a fog, she turned and again took in her own huge living room. Her china cup was no longer sitting on the end table near the couch where she'd set it between sips.

This was all too real.

"You need to wake up," she said out loud.

She heard a knock. When she looked behind her, she found a black, arched door that wasn't there before.

Lightning flashed, blinding her momentarily. Thunder clashed within seconds.

Now, something was pounding at the door.

The sound echoed through the room, overriding the inviting crackle of the fire in the hearth. On a normal day, a knock on her door wouldn't feel threatening, but this entire dream situation was just *wrong*. This felt real; it didn't feel like a dream. If it was, Sara knew she'd somehow dreamed herself into a horror flick.

"It's a monster. Don't open it." Sara whispered to herself.

Another roar of thunder replied. Sara stared at the flames in the hearth as she shimmied from the ottoman and snuggled as deep as possible into the chair. She used the green plaid throw to cover up, trying to hide like a child hiding under the covers on the bed. Her heart pounded in her chest, and cold reached into her soul like a hand grabbing hold. She didn't like this dream, and she didn't like this dream room anymore.

She heard a voice like a whisper coming from outside the door. It called her name. "Sara..."

The door vibrated with more pounding. The voice penetrated the sound of the storm. "Open the door! Let me in!"

She clenched her jaw and didn't reply her thought, *go away!* She thought it best she stayed quiet and didn't let the monster know she was there, trying to hide.

Her open book slid to the floor with a plop.

"I know you're in there! Let me in!" Now the voice sounded coaxing.

"Wake up, Sara," she whispered.

She reached over and pinched the tender, underside of her opposite arm, sending pain in a zing up to her shoulder before it faded.

The dream room disappeared.

Sara sat up on her own sofa. Morning light blinded her. Considering the heavy feeling that filled her, she was certain she'd run a marathon all night instead of sleeping.

Fighting down the shiver that snaked up her back, she climbed off the couch and crossed the room to her bookshelf. The light was still on inside the miniature room. And now, there was an arched, black door on the back wall. A tiny green plaid cover looped over the arm of the chair. A miniature version of her favorite tea cup sat on the side table. The miniature book lying on the floor was face down, and the print of the back-cover blurb was too small to read. She looked around her living room. Her plaid throw, book and tea cup were no longer there.

"Impossible."

Sara flipped the light switch which still rested on the book next to the dream room box, and the little room went dark.

She knew it was a senseless move, but she grabbed a large nearby book anyway, and placed it in front of the opening to the tiny room, as if it might be enough to hold whatever evil monster might be lurking in that room.

"There's no monster," she said out loud, straightening her shoulders. "At least not in that little room."

Her long, hot shower didn't wash away the fuzzy fear that lingered. Telling herself it had to have been a dream didn't help much, either.

She forced the idea of the dream from her thoughts. Or tried to, anyway. She turned to her research of a list of unsolved crimes she could use for future podcasts, but it was impossible for her to focus.

She stepped away from her computer and gulped down a big glass of water, hoping to wash away the cold feeling loitering in her gut. She considered another pot of hot tea, but after losing one much-loved china teacup to a miniature room, she was hesitant to make another.

The early spring sun warmed her skin as she ventured on a walk through the park, but the fresh air did nothing to shake off the fog that clouded her. By mid-afternoon, she gave into the need for a nap. She lay down on her bed, down the hall and rooms away from the miniature room. She promised herself after a little rest, she would at least find a topic for her next broadcast.

She shuddered when she woke to discover she was back inside the dream room on her own bookshelf.

She could see little but dark shadows because the light was off. There was no fire in the hearth. She didn't have light from her living room, either, because she'd placed a book in front of it.

A whisper came from a far corner of the small room. "You should have let me in, Sara. This would have been so much easier."

"What would have?" she couldn't help but ask.

"Working my way in like this just takes a little more effort and energy on my part."

The three miniature tapers in the candelabra flickered to life, casting glowing light into the small space.

The bookstore owner who rang up her purchase at the bookstore sat in the red chair, his legs on the ottoman as if he owned the place But then, she thought, perhaps he somehow did.

The room was as it had been when she looked at it earlier that morning—the green blanket over the arm of the chair, her teacup on the table, and her book on the floor.

"Nick?"

Sara recognized it had been his voice she'd heard through the storm last night.

"Why the hell would I dream about you?" she continued.

He met her gaze and smiled.

It made her feel like a mouse being toyed with by a cat.

"I command you to dream about me. This is a dream I weave. And I'm going to enjoy you the best in this, your dream room, before I kill you."

His words sent icy terror to her heart. She'd told herself there was no monster knocking at the door of her dream room. She'd been wrong; there was a monster. And he'd managed to slither into her dream world.

"Why is that?" Sara forced her voice to remain calm and even despite the fact she felt as if she was floating, or perhaps watching what she was experiencing through someone else's eyes. All of this felt real and surreal at the same time.

"You're the first one who didn't let me in when I knocked. Danielle and Tanya both opened the door before I even called to them. Sweet little Kat, the one who actually purred as I strangled her—opened the door the moment I called, 'here, kitty, kitty, kitty.'"

He was tall and lanky and sitting in the red chair, he barely had to raise his chin to look at her. "Do you have any idea what it takes to invade someone's dream?"

She played along. "Nope. Why don't you tell me."

Her knees weak, she considered pulling the ottoman out from under his feet so she could sit on it. But keeping as much distance as possible between herself and him seemed like a good idea. She considered running through that arched doorway, but she had no idea where she might end up if she did. Would she face plant against the back of her book shelf? She wasn't so certain she wanted to find out.

"I always thought I heard voices," he explained, crossing his arms. "I was afraid I might be insane."

Sara didn't voice it, but she was certain he was.

He continued. "What I heard was thoughts of people around me. I heard you as you waited in line thinking your favorite author, Simon Dare, is hot. I assure you he's far from it. In fact, I found him to be a bit of a wimp. He was a boring speaker. I heard him once, last year. I tried to get close enough to him to hear his thoughts. But he was surrounded by horny, needy women. I couldn't get within twenty feet."

"Too bad for you," Sara put in, still working to calm her heart. And now that she knew what he could do—if it were true—she tried to shield her mind, empty her thoughts so he didn't know how terrified she was. He was already at an advantage getting into her dream and into her dream room. She had no idea how he could go from hearing the thoughts of others to slipping into their dreams.

He raised his eyebrows. "Now I'm able to take my ability to a new level and show up in a dream room where I can be a part of your dream. At first, I just spent time in dreams. But, boy, is that boring."

"I'll bet."

"I mean, just how long do you think we can talk about Simon Dare?" Nick gave an absent wave to the book on the floor. "And then I found out I could make people do things in the dreams we shared, like dance naked. When I perfected that, I shared a dream with a bitchy cheerleader I knew from high school where I made her have sex with me for hours."

Oh, I'm so in trouble.

"So, what are you thinking now, sweet, pretty Sara?" Nick asked, sitting forward, his gaze sharpening on her face, "because, oddly, I hear nothing. I don't even sense your fear, even though I'm sure it's seeping into every joint of your body as you come to the realization you're conversing with the man who's going to watch the life fade from your eyes. And do you know the best part?"

There was a *best part?*

"Do share." Sara didn't trust herself to say more than two or three words at a time, for fear he would hear her terror in the way she couldn't keep her words even. She pinched herself on the arm as she'd done to end the previous trip into her dream room.

This time, the pain didn't wake her. She remained standing about three feet from a serial killer who hadn't seen her action and continued with his soul-freezing explanation. She needed to think of another way to escape this nightmare.

"None of the cops who investigated my victims can figure it out. Except maybe that Grayson guy. He investigated two of my girls. I thought I'd better watch him. So, I did, with a pair of binoculars. He lingered longer over my kitty cat's body, almost as if he could see something that wasn't there. It's too bad our dream died when she did, or I could have watched him from our dream room." He paused as if searching for something more.

Then his gaze focused, he and went on. "I can kill and not leave a single trace of evidence. What a weapon. I should apply at the CIA; just think of what I could do."

Sara was still doing her best to not think at all, to keep her mind closed and empty. "Yes, perhaps you should go do that instead of killing innocent women."

"You've never hunted for sport, have you?"

"I've always been partial to synchronized swimming," she replied.

He laughed hard. "Ah, and this time I picked a woman with a sense of humor. I love it. You and I are going to have so much fun. I'm going to enjoy breaking you."

For some odd reason, when he said the word breaking, Sara's attention shifted to the tea cup on the table. She'd never know if he caught a grasp of her thoughts or he just knew he needed to move. Not that it mattered. What mattered was she managed to grab the teacup just before he jumped out of the chair and rushed her. It was his action, knocking her to the carpet, that caused the cup to break against the corner of the table. Shards of cup fell to the floor as she did. One, or perhaps two, of the three pieces gripped in her fist managed to cut her palm.

Sara fought to ignore the pain, fought against the reflex to open her hand, and fought against her assailant who pressed on top of her as she felt soft carpet cushion the back of her head.

Working to act without thinking so he wouldn't know her plans, she brought a knee up between his legs.

The groan of pain that escaped him was music to her ears.

She wasted no time slashing the side of his face, down from his right eye with a piece of the broken tea cup. She couldn't help but think her mother would have been proud to know the final use of her favorite cup.

There was a split second of time she felt the warmth of his blood land on her face before she woke on the floor in her own bedroom.

Her hand was bleeding. When she rushed to the bathroom to place it under cool, running water from the sink, she looked up at her own reflection in the mirror to find very real blood splatter on her face.

Chapter Two

Detective Tony Grayson stepped into *Signorino's Bakery and Brew*. The place bustled with activity. There was a busload of tourists heading on a springtime ghost hunt at a nearby 'closed' insane asylum, and they were stopping at the now famous Marston's Tunnel a few miles away. The twenty-something ghost hunters were first enjoying Lizzy Signorino's coffee and pastries.

The Ladies' Auxiliary had a table set up near the door asking for donations for the upcoming annual Easter egg hunt. Tony gave them a generous donation. In return, they gave him an ink pen, a back scratcher, and a small sewing kit complete with two needles, five different colors of thread, a little pair of scissors, a needle threader, and a thimble. He placed the items into his pocket before ordering his coffee.

Within minutes, he was seated at a table taking in all the activity and enjoying the sense of community.

Since moving to town and spending nearly every morning in the coffee shop, he'd learned even without a bus load of travelers, the coffee shop was hopping. It was the place to be in Mossy Point.

A young woman slipped into the chair across from him. She appeared disheveled and uncertain. Drugs? Alcohol? Years of experience told him no. Her gray eyes looked tired and were underlined by dark circles, but clear. He spent another moment or two studying her. She clasped her hands on the table in front of her, but fidgeted with her fingers, obviously nervous. Years of experience also told him cops made people nervous, even when police assistance was necessary. He forced himself to take a slow sip of his coffee before addressing her. "Can I help you?"

"You're Detective Tony Grayson?"

He held her gaze. "Who's asking?"

"Sara Greene." As if she realized her hands gave away her nervousness, she clasped them in her lap, out of sight.

"Can I buy you a coffee, Sara Greene?"

"Thank you."

Her voice was deep, smooth, and a little throaty. He tried to place where he'd heard that voice before. It would eventually come to him.

Tony flagged over Amanda, the new morning waitress, and listened as Sara Greene ordered a large double expresso. She didn't plan on sleeping any time soon.

He waited until Amanda left to quietly ask, "Are you in trouble, Sara?"

"Yes."

"You could come with me to the station and make a full report."

She shifted in her chair. "I don't know what he can see, so I need to be careful where I go."

Stalker? Abusive significant other? "He?" Tony asked.

She looked around, and he allowed her the time. He didn't push. Experience taught him patience. He looked around the coffee shop, too, taking in faces, securing them to memory, just in case her *he* was there.

After several minutes, she spoke. "Two towns over, there's a new shop called the Nick and Cranny Book Store."

"I don't know about it, but that's okay." He kept his tone even, calm. "What about it?"

"The owner, his name is Nick."

"Go figure. Nick, what?"

Her shoulders hunched. "I don't know his last name."

Tony recognized fear in her eyes. "Has he threatened you?"

"Yes, but it's not what you think."

"Not what I think?" That was a new one. A threat was a threat.

"Just listen. Please. I know this is going to sound really crazy. So, please, just listen."

The desperation in her voice mixed like oil and vinegar with the fear in her eyes. "All right."

She paused as Amanda placed her expresso on the table in front of her. "Can I get you anything else?" Amanda asked with a smile.

Sara mumbled, "No, thank you."

But Tony added, "Bring her a couple of those shortbread cookies, please."

"Sure thing," replied Amanda, before she strode off to get them.

Once she was gone, Sarah said, "Thank you, but—"

"You look like you could use a little sugar," Tony interrupted.

"Okay."

Tony took a long swallow of his cooling coffee, working to appear as if he had all the time in the world. "Please continue. If this Nick guy isn't threatening you, what's he doing?"

"Killing," she replied.

Her single word made him pause in taking another drink of coffee. "Killing who?"

"Those women, the ones found dead in their beds, for no apparent reason, all young and in good health. He told me them by name—Danielle, Tanya, and Kathryn Mertah, he called her Kat, his kitty cat.'"

"When did he tell you this?"

She didn't reply because Amanda brought a plate with three cookies on it and set it in front of Sara. "Thank you," Sara said.

"Can I get you anything else?" Amanda asked again.

"No, thank you."

Sara took a bite of a cookie and washed it down with a sip of coffee before she continued. "In his book store, he sells these little miniature boxes that look like narrow single rooms of a doll house. He called them dream rooms. They go on a bookshelf. He was giving them away for free and I chose one. I put it on my bookshelf. I fell asleep on my couch, reading the latest true crime book I bought. I woke up, and it was like I'd managed to shrink myself down to this big."

She held up her finger and her thumb with approximately three inches between them.

"And I was in that room. I actually could look out the open end of that dream room and see my giant couch, my living room. It was overwhelming, like a sucker punch to the gut. And the dream room had a door on the inner corner, a black door, even though there was no door when I brought it home." She shivered, clasping her hands around her cup. "Rain beat against the window. Then there was a loud pounding, something, someone knocking at the door. I knew it had to be a monster, so I curled up under the blanket on the chair and didn't answer."

Tony took another sip, waiting, so she went on.

"I pinched my own arm to wake up, and I did. Although I was exhausted, as if I hadn't slept in three days."

Tony didn't interrupt just listened to every word.

She paused and studied him. "I know what you're thinking, that it was just a dream. I did that, too, that first day. But the second time I went to sleep—which I want you to know was on my bed, in my bedroom, rooms away from that dream room on my shelf—I was once again in that miniature room. And Nick, the guy who rang up my sale at the book store, the owner, was there with me." She paused to take another sip before continuing. "He told me how he could hear people's thoughts. Then he told me how that ability increased and grew and allowed him to get into someone's dreams, where he made people do things. He said he even made some woman from his high school days have sex with him. And he said he killed those women in their dreams. I did some research, and there really is something called a—"

"A dream walker," Tony interrupted. "Somone who can walk into the dreams of others." He'd done his own research. Number one, he'd had his own experience. Number two, he'd had a previous case where he was able to dream about a murder before it actually happened.

"Yes, but there's also something called a dream weaver, which is a person who can also create or affect events within a dream."

Tony knew about that, too, because he'd been afraid he was the dream weaver in that case and he was creating the murder by manipulating the dreams of the murderer. He held her gaze and asked, "Even though I won't dispute those two things exist, why should I believe what you experienced wasn't just a dream? Or, two dreams?"

She took a deep breath and glanced about the room, taking in the activity as if to make certain no one was listening. "Number one, before I fell asleep, I was drinking tea out of my mother's favorite tea cup, which was next to me on the side table at the end of the couch. When I was in the dream room, the tea cup was there, only now it's this big." Again, she held up a finger and thumb spanning about a half inch between. "And it's no longer on my end table. It actually even had my tea still in it, I could smell it. When he grabbed me and knocked me to the floor, I managed to grab the teacup and break it."

She took a slow swallow of her coffee as if she needed to calm herself. Tony, too, took a drink.

"The broken china cut my hand."

She held up her hand, revealing the adhesive bandage on her palm. "I have four stitches. I was also able to grab a big triangular piece and cut him, too. I sliced him down his face from here to here, down his eye." She moved a finger from just above her right eye brow to the middle of her cheek. "I believe it was what broke his dream hold over me and freed me. I woke up on the floor beside my bed, my hand bleeding on the rug. And I had his blood on my face. Before coming here to find you, I went to the bookstore. Nick, the owner, has a bandage over part of his face and his eye. And that's not all."

"There's more?" The coffee in Tony's stomach churned as if someone had set it to percolate. Either she was telling him the craziest, most insane story ever, or he was dealing with a killer unlike any other he'd ever known. He didn't like either scenario. It took everything he possessed to keep his face free from any reaction, but he couldn't hide from the familiarity of it.

"He mentioned you by name. When he talked about Kathryn Mertah, calling her his kitty cat, he said the other investigators were too stupid to catch him, but he was worried about you, Detective Grayson. He watched you with a pair of binoculars. He said he could no longer be in her dream room, that since she was dead, the dream died with her. He still thought you lingered in Kathryn Mertah's apartment longer than any of the others. He was concerned perhaps you could see something you shouldn't be able to see."

Tony sucked in a breath and remembered the feeling that filled him as he walked around Kathryn Mertah's bedroom, as if he wasn't alone, as if he was being watched. He remembered feeling that same cold feeling as a child, but at the time, he'd washed that feeling away with a hot slug of bitter coffee. He didn't mention to Sara he'd studied one of the miniature rooms on her bookshelf. He also didn't mention that the tiny room was a mess with both the table and chair turned on their sides and broken tiny dishes, as if there had been a struggle there. At the time, he'd been struck by the oddness of having a miniature room that looked like that. He made a mental note to call Kathryn's family and ask about that belonging. Not that he could use it as evidence. No jury in the world would convict someone based on broken dollhouse furniture. But at least he would know.

Right now, he fought to stop the cold, quiver of fear that filled his gut. When he took a drink of his coffee, he found it too cool to warm him. "I'd like to see this little dream room of yours."

"Okay."

As he followed Sara Greene to her house, he called the Chief of Police to let him know he was working on a follow up and wouldn't be back to his office just yet. Tony got his job done and often had time to help his fellow patrolmen keep the streets of Mossy Point and the surrounding area safe, so the Chief pretty much let him work at his own pace.

Sara's house turned out to be a smaller, older house on the south side of town, not far from the old mill building he now owned and was renovating. He couldn't help but notice the strong smell of coffee. "Have you been drinking a lot of coffee?" he asked as she closed the door behind him.

"I've been awake for—" she looked at the fitness watch on her wrist—"almost thirty-one hours now. I'm terrified to fall asleep. At the same time, I'm afraid to stay awake, afraid that when I'm finally unable to keep myself awake any longer, I'll be so exhausted, I can't fight him off or I can't wake up. Not that I could wake myself before until my cutting him broke his connection or whatever. I just don't know what to do."

He looked around, taking in details of her space. "What do you do for a living?"

"I run a podcast, which is one of the reasons I was hesitant to come talk to you, or anyone."

"Oh? What kind of podcast?"

She shrugged. "Unsolved mysteries and crimes. It's called The Unsolved Abyss."

He offered her a grin. "I thought I recognized your voice." He didn't tell her he thought she had the dreamiest, sexiest voice.

"You listen to it?"

"When I can. Show me your little room."

She led him into the living room. He took it all in at once, the comfortable couch, the bookshelves, the TV on a table in the corner, and the gas fireplace. There was a soft scent of lavender in the air. The room had a feel of home, and it was something he missed since his divorce, something he hoped to regain as he renovated his new home.

On the bookshelf, she turned a small wired switch and lit up the miniature dream room she'd gotten at the bookstore. Like the living room, Tony took it all in at once, seeing the chair she described, the table, the plaid coverlet that looked to be about three inches square, as well as broken pieces of china on the miniature carpeted floor.

"Have you thought about busting it with a hammer?" he asked.

"Yes, I have, but I'm afraid it isn't the dream room that holds me to him. If I smash it, I don't know where that will put me. At least this little dream room is in my house in a familiar place."

"What do you think holds you to him?"

"He touched my hand." Sara shook her head. "It was just a simple touch after I paid, but it left me cold."

"Do you have a pair of tweezers and a bottle of alcohol and a flashlight?" he asked.

She was gone for a moment as she retrieved them.

While she was out of the room, he took the tiny sewing kit from his pocket and retrieved one of the two sewing needles. Carefully, he placed the needle on the carpet next to the red chair, opposite from the broken tea cup. With one finger, he rolled the needle out of sight under the miniature chair. The ruffle at the bottom of the chair hid it completely. He had no idea what this killer could see or if he could see anything or everything Sara saw. He didn't know this killer's capabilities or even how true any of this story was.

But looking at Sara, he knew she believed it.

And it was his job to protect her.

For the past two years, he'd listened to her voice on her podcast, listened to her deductions and her reasoning when it came to mysteries. She wasn't insane. She was a levelheaded young woman. And he had the idea she didn't have much time. Sooner rather than later, she was going to need to sleep. He needed to do everything he could to help her defeat this killer before she was forced to face him.

She returned with his requested objects. He asked her to hold the light and shine it on the small broken tea cup pieces. There was clearly something on them, but it appeared to be brown. There were also spots on the carpet.

"Do you know which might have his blood on it?"

This might be a waste of his time, but he really needed to know. He knew if he was back in the city and shared this with his captain, the old chump would say Sara Greene staged this for attention, created this for her podcast. He was a detective because that's what he did, he investigated, and he found answers. To find answers, he needed to search for evidence. This was evidence.

"I know the piece I cut him with was a triangle." She pointed. "That piece right there is the only triangle."

After cleaning the tweezers with alcohol, he gently grasped the piece and carefully placed it into a small, self-closing evidence bag.

For grins and groans, he took a second, smaller piece and placed it into a second bag.

"How awake are you?"

"I'm okay right now."

He smiled. "Take a ride with me."

They stepped outside onto Sara's small porch. Tony thought the crafty welcome sign with flowers and the comfortable-looking rocking chairs were nice. The building clouds told him more storms were rolling in. Sitting out on this porch watching the rain sounded like a great way to spend a day.

But first he had a job to do.

"Sara?" he whispered.

She turned to him after she locked the front door.

He leaned in close, hating to invade her personal space. Nick had already invaded her.

"I don't know what or how much he can see or hear. I think the dream is his dream; that's why things show up, like the door. I don't think you can dream in a weapon to defend yourself, and I think if you try to use something he put in there, like the candle stick holder or the fireplace poker, he'll dream it away. So, I hid something in there; don't hesitate to use it. I'm sure he won't hesitate." He didn't add he planned to try to get into her dream room, too, to help her, but he wasn't sure he could. He didn't share with her his thought that Nick had to be very powerful in his ability if he could take things from the real world and put them into a dream world.

She studied him for a long moment. "You really believe me?"

"Let's just say in my job, I've learned it's not all black and white. There are a lot of gray areas, and a lot of things that happen that can't always be explained in a report." That was all he chose to share with her. He didn't need to share any of his childhood experiences with her. At least not now, not yet. She had other things on her mind, other things she needed to face.

"Where are we going?" she asked.

He held up a finger to keep her quiet, the signal to wait. "I'll need you to trust me."

Neither spoke during the drive. He drove them to the lab, where he greeted his best lab guy, Benny. "Hey, Benny." He introduced Sara and explained he was helping her out with a domestic, personal matter "Can you check something for me off the record?"

Benny, a tall, thin man dressed in a white lab coat, rubbed his long fingers together. "Oh, I love off the record. It sounds so cloak and dagger."

Tony grinned. "You have no idea."

It was sometime later that Benny exclaimed, "Wow, dollhouse china, who'd a thought? And, boy, somebody had to have paid an arm and a leg for this."

"Why do you say that?"

"Take a look for yourself." He put the magnetized image on the big screen on the wall. "We can clearly see the china watermark. That's some nice, expensive stuff. My mom always wanted a set of that, but none of us can afford it. Wait until I tell her she can get a dollhouse set."

"What can you tell us about the blood?"

"There are two different types, both definitely human. One is AB positive; the other is O positive."

As they walked back out into the dreary spring day, Sara commented, "I'm AB positive. But even if we could prove or conclude Bookstore Nick is O positive, we can't use any of that for evidence, right?"

Tony nodded. "Right."

"Why, then, did we just waste this time?"

"For me. I needed to know for me."

"Where are we going now?" she asked as he unlocked the car doors.

"To get something to eat."

"If I get full and happy, it'll be harder for me to stay awake," she reminded him.

"You're going to have to sleep sometime, and I want you to be strong and quick when you have to face him."

"You have no doubt?"

He waited until they were both tucked warm and dry into his car and belted in before he replied. "When I was a kid, something happened." He started the car.

"What?"

"I was raised in a sheltered home with no rated R movies. My parents didn't cuss, or drink, or smoke. We prayed before meals and went to church every Sunday. My parents weren't fanatics, but they raised us on the strong sense of right and wrong. So, when I started having these nightmares about the school custodian, in the dark, creepy science lab at school, I thought like any other ten-year-old. I figured I must have done some sort of sin. The nightmares were certainly sinful with this older man wanting me to touch him. My parents, of course, questioned why I suddenly wasn't sleeping at night. My grades were beginning to slip, and I couldn't stay awake in class. I was sleep deprived and feeling horrible when the new young principal, Mr. Huffman, called me into his office. I never planned to tell. I guess by then I was out of my mind from lack of sleep, and I told him everything. I expected him to call in the guys in the white coats. At the very least, I expected some sort of therapy. I think back then a lot of kids were getting 'therapy.' But that wasn't what happened. He let me take a nap on the couch in his office. I think it was the first three hours of uninterrupted sleep I'd had in a long time. I remember thinking I might cry I felt so much better, or I might cry simply because he listened to me. He woke me up in time for me to go home at the end of the day, and he told me to go to bed at the normal time and not be afraid to sleep. He told me it would be okay, that he'd fix it, and that I could trust him.

"I didn't understand any of that, but I felt so much better after my nap that I believed him. I felt like I could trust him. At least until I went to sleep and woke up in the dark, creepy science lab again, with Mr. Straker, the custodian there. I can't even begin to describe the betrayal I felt. I thought I was going to just crawl into a ball on the floor and cry, but then Mr. Huffman was there, in the dream with me, with us. I don't remember much about what happened because Mr. Huffman told me stay behind him, and to cover my ears and not look. But I do remember Mr. Huffman saying it was time for Mr. Straker to stop. I think he had a gun, but I didn't see it because I did what he said and didn't look. But Straker said, 'You can't use that in this dream world. It's a world I created.' And Mr. Huffman said, 'But I can, because I put it in here and it isn't part of your dream creation.'

"There was a loud bang. Mr. Huffman grabbed my hand, and I woke up. I was in my bed, and I was safe. And when I went to school the next day, everyone was sorry and sad because they said Mr. Straker, the custodian, must have had a heart attack in his sleep, and he was dead. There was a big funeral, and they talked about all of his years of service.

I just remember looking at Mr. Huffman. He was looking at me, and there was this unspoken communication between us.

"I never talked about it again. But I got some sleep. I got my grades up again, and got back to my usual self. When I was in eighth grade and had access to the internet without someone looking over my shoulder for fear I'd check out all the porn sights, I searched dream killers and learned about dream weavers and dream walkers. I actually forgot about all that until I was standing there in Kathryn Mertah's bedroom, and there was no evident cause of death. And the ME said it was like she had a heart attack in her sleep. It flooded back and made me shiver. When you came and sat at my table, I had actually just looked up Mr. Huffman."

"Where is he now?" Sara asked.

"He's still the principal, sitting in the same office where I told him about my nightmares."

"What are we waiting for?"

"Let's take him some lunch." Tony turned at the next street, and they went through a fast-food drive-in in silence.

Except for gray hair and few wrinkles, Mr. Huffman hadn't changed much. His blue eyes were still kind and inquisitive and knowing. "Hello, Tony," he said after Tony and Sara were ushered into his office.

Tony was certain the moment he stepped through the doors of the school, he'd stepped back in time. The only thing different was now he had called ahead and he had to ring a bell and be admitted by someone who unlocked the door. The bulletin board was decorated with spring flowers. A strong smell of marker filled the hall. Muffled voices murmured from nearby classes.

Mr. Huffman had a different secretary, and the desk plate read Barbara Phillips.

There were only a few things in Mr. Huffman's office that had changed. The couch where Tony had taken that wonderful afternoon nap was now blue and not brown. When Tony sat in the sturdy wooden chair opposite Mr. Huffman now, he thought the chair had somehow shrunk. But he was pretty certain it was the same chair. As Mr. Huffman closed the door and a distinct, audible click sounded through the office, a sense of déjà vu washed through him. Again, he was a little terrified by a nightmare he couldn't escape.

He forced down a swallow and cleared his throat, working to convince himself he was no longer that scared little boy. He was a seasoned cop with a badge and gun, and he knew how to use both of them.

Tony introduced Sara.

"You didn't go to school here," Mr. Huffman remarked. He laced his fingers and placed his hands on the organized desk before him, studying Sara. "I would remember you."

"I'll bet you would," she said with a smile. "No, I didn't. I did my grade school years at Unit 77."

"Ah, home of the Eagles."

"Yes."

He turned to Tony. "You know, Tony, all these years, I expected you to come here. I'm surprised we never had a conversation sooner. In fact, we hardly talked at all after—"

"I know how you stopped him," Tony interrupted him. "You placed something into the room, something he didn't dream there, something he couldn't dream away. You used it to kill him."

Mr. Huffman's demeanor hardened as he met Tony's gaze. "I used it to stop him. Would you rather I hadn't?"

"No. I'm glad you did."

The other man nodded. "And if you're here to arrest me now that you're the law, I'll deny everything. I'm not even sure I remember ever having you in my office when you were a student here. But I'm proud of the fine, outstanding citizen you've become."

"Mr. Huffman, I'm not here to arrest you. And Sara isn't a cop. I need to know how you did it. How you got into that dream."

Mr. Huffman was quiet for a long moment. "I think you're old enough to call me Randy, don't you?"

"Whatever," Tony let out, working to curb his anger. Time was wasting, and he hadn't missed the yawn Sara worked to hide. "I need to know how you got in the dream, *Randy*."

Recognition spread across Randy's expression. "That rash of young women who all died in their sleep? You think..."

"No, I don't think. I know."

Randy looked at Sara. "Someone's plaguing you?"

"Well, it's more like he's terrorizing me but, yes, the owner of the bookstore is plaguing me. And he's killed others. I managed to wake up and escape him before I was next on his list."

Tony interrupted. "I did what you did. I put something into the room where he dreams her to, but I'm worried it won't be enough, that he'll be too quick for her, especially since she's tired. I need to get into the dream and help her. How do I do it?"

The principal sighed. "It's a little hard to explain. Showing you will be much easier, so I'll need to be where the dream takes place. But there's something you have to do first."

Tony met Randy's gaze. "What?"

"You have to touch him."

The room was completely quiet for a long moment as everyone digested that knowledge.

"Touch him?" Tony asked.

"I don't care how you do it, but you need to get to the bookstore and brush up against him, or take a book out of his hand, or tap him on the shoulder. You can even help him take a piss if you want, I don't care, but you have to make contact with him, preferably skin-to-skin, just as I'm sure he made with Sara to get her into the dream he created. And it would help if you could get to sleep by midnight. At midnight, the wall between reality and the other world is thinnest, so that would help." He paused. "And, Tony?"

"What?"

"You have to be careful."

Tony met his gaze. "I will."

"You don't understand. You touch him, you can invade his dream. But it's the same with his touching you. He can weave an entirely new dream for you and put you somewhere else."

"That makes me feel all warm and fuzzy inside," Tony replied, not even trying to hold back the sarcasm. He didn't add that if Nick planned or tried to kill him, as Nick had killed so many other women, he'd better do it on the first try.

Even though Sara was yawning, Tony was certain tiny jolts of electricity were charging through his body, and he doubted he could get to sleep without the help of a lot of alcohol or a drug or two.

Randy offered him a grin Tony thought was out of place. "Why don't you leave Sara here? She can take a nap on my old sofa over there. If he's at the bookstore working, he won't be sleeping, so she should be safe while you go to the bookstore and pick me up the latest true crime book by Simon Dare."

"You read Simon Dare?" Sara asked. "I love him."

"Doesn't everyone?" Randy asked in return. He looked at Tony, and his expression became stern. "Time's wasting."

Tony turned to Sara, eyebrows raised. "Are you okay if I leave?"

Sara looked at Randy. "Can we trust him?" she asked.

"I trusted him as a kid, and I trusted him enough to bring you to him for help," Tony replied. "If I find out I can't trust him, I'll kill him at the first opportunity."

They spoke as if Randy wasn't sitting right there in front of them hearing every word. Randy stared hard at them in return before he spoke. "I will not let anything happen to her."

"Okay, I'll stay," Sara attempted to assure him.

Tony didn't like the idea of her taking a nap where he couldn't be there to wake her up. He wasn't even certain he would know if he needed to wake her or if shaking her would be enough. But he wasn't about to be seen with her at the bookstore. And having her sleep away from that little dream room while Nick was working and not able to sleep did sound like the safest move. None of that made leaving her any easier.

Thunder rumbled and distant lightning split the sky as another storm rolled in. The starting rain sent the bad traffic level up about seven or eight notches. Tony touched base with his chief, Mac, to let him know he wouldn't be into the office today but was following some leads. Mac was a good guy, who trusted his gut, and allowed Tony the freedom to trust his own.

He felt his heart pounding in his chest as he rushed through the door of the bookstore, doing his best to dodge the rain, and failing at it. He didn't want to just touch Nick, he wanted to punch his lights out, slap a pair of cuffs on him, and drag his ass to the nearest cell. But he knew from his own experience with a dream weaver that would never stop him. Besides, he had no legitimate reason to arrest Bookstore Nick or hold him, and he had no evidence at all, no matter what he knew or suspected about Nick.

Nick was easy to find, given the white gauze taped to the right side of his face.

Chapter Three

Sara woke from a dreamless nap, feeling groggy and disoriented. It took several blinking moments to recognize Randy's office. She was alone, the lights were dimmed, rain drummed against the nearby window sill. She should be hungry, she thought. She should, at least, feel thirsty, but she didn't. It was as if Nick had somehow managed to become so woven into her subconscious, he had the ability to suck all feeling and life and even basic need from her. The door opened and Tony and Randy returned.

Maybe not all life was sucked out of her, because she could swear her heart felt lighter seeing Tony was back safe. She sat up, placed her feet on the floor, every joint feeling stiff, as if she was trying to find the downhill side of a bad bout of the flu.

Tony sat down beside her. "Do you feel better since you slept?"

"Actually, no,"

Randy carried a tray. "The weaver lives and grows stronger off your energy. I brought you something to eat. It should help. Besides, the cafeteria food here isn't too bad."

"I'm not very hungry."

"Yes, he robs you of that, too. Try and eat something anyway." Randy set the tray on the table before her where she saw he brought her a peanut butter and jelly sandwich with apple slices and a small carton of milk.

Sara took a bite to appease him, finding it didn't taste like cardboard, as she imagined. "Tell me you managed to touch him," she said to Tony.

"Oh, I managed more than that. I bumped into that poor sap carrying an extra-large cup of extra hot coffee. It was such a terrible accident." He feigned sympathy. "I told him over and over how sorry I was. It's too bad he may have a few burns to go along with the cut you gave him. I had to help him brush some hot coffee off his face right over the bandage he had there. I certainly hope my action didn't hurt too much."

Perhaps Nick hadn't managed to suck all the feeling out of her, because Sara laughed.

Later, after the darkness covered her little house, with the rain still beating against the windows and lightning flashing every few seconds, the three of them settled into the living room. Sara attempted to warm her insides with a cup of hot tea, but was unsuccessful. She'd made coffee for Tony and Randy, but she couldn't help but notice Tony's sat untouched and cooling on the coffee table. Every now and then, the lights blinked, thanks to the storm.

Sara lit several different sized candles that decorated the hearth. Tony came up behind her.

"That looks nice," he commented. "It gives the room a special...warmth."

Sara chuckled. "It does. The next guy who hosts my true crime podcast after I'm dead can entitle my case *Death by Candlelight*."

"How about you do the podcast, but keep the title? I like it. I'll be listening to it when *you* broadcast it."

Sara shivered. "I have to get through this first."

"And you will. *We* will."

Randy was the only one who didn't appear worried or nervous. Sara wondered if it was because he'd dealt with this before or if he was just really good at hiding his concern. There were so many tornadoes touching down within her. She felt as if something burned and churned in her gut, but goosebumps covered her arms. Her insides pulsed with what felt like jolts of electrical current. At the same time, Tony's closeness seemed to calm her.

She wanted to trust him.

But it wasn't easy. She knew the terror of being inside that tiny room with Nick telling her how he planned to kill her. And, of course, now he was more than just a serial killer. Now, he was a pissed-off serial killer.

Randy studied the little bookshelf room.

"What? You're thinking something," Sara said.

Randy met her gaze. "I find it odd he can, or does even, dream you into something like a little dollhouse room. Why not just dream you into your living room?"

"He's afraid of leaving evidence in a bigger room," Tony put in. "He got cut on a broken piece of teacup. If that dream had been in the real living room, his evidence would have been here. I could have used it against him. Even if it had only been a dream, it's still evidence."

Sara was certain an entire colony of ants scurried around in her stomach. She had no idea how she was expected to sleep, much less even relax enough to sleep. At the same time, the evening seemed to drag. Midnight felt hours away.

"What happens if he decides to do something different besides enter my dream room?"

"Like what?" Randy asked.

"Like actually come here to my house while Tony and I are asleep and waiting for him in my dream."

"I'll be awake. I'll be watching," Randy said.

"And if he kills you?"

"The fact he's a dream weaver tells me his power is only in the dream realm." Randy turned his attention to Tony. "How was he when you spilled your coffee on him?"

"He was having a hard time not crying."

"Not even cussing?" Randy asked.

"No."

"Did he even call you out on it with, 'hey, man, why the fuck don't you watch where you're going?'"

Tony grinned. "Nope. Just started shaking his arm off and brushing at his face, and ran in the direction of the bathrooms."

"The typical person, like you, Sara, and me, would cuss if coffee spilled. We'd probably at the very least mutter an *oh, shit* or something equivalent. Tony here would probably say something a bit stronger and for way longer." He glanced at Sara, then Tony. "But Tony, if you remember Garrett Straker, the custodian who was weaving your nightmare, he wouldn't—and, actually, couldn't—hurt anyone when he was in wakeville. He may have even wanted to, but he could only let loose the evil when he was in a dream. If I'd exposed him in any way back then, even if there had been some sort of proof, no one, not anyone who actually knew him, would believe it. He was a church-going, easy-going guy who comforted kids after they puked and never raised his voice to anyone, not even his wife."

"Why did you believe me so easily when I came to you all those years ago?" Tony frowned. "I didn't think anyone would believe me, and I was certain my parents would have just sent me to some head shrinker somewhere to try and get rid of my bad dreams. Knowing what I know now, someone even would have tried to pin it on one of my parents or a relative, saying someone abused me and I've buried it so deep that it's coming out in my dreams. But you didn't even question it. You just told me to not to worry about sleeping that night, that you'd fix it."

"It's hard to say. I saw your fear. In my career, I've learned to listen to kids more than adults, especially when most adults don't think they need to listen to kids. I knew you weren't lying. And..." Randy paused. "You weren't the first to tell me a story about Garrett Straker. In fact, you were the third. I knew it was time to do something about it. Unfortunately, he wasn't like another unruly child I could threaten or dish out a punishment or send to detention."

"There's only one way to stop him, isn't there?" Sara asked.

Randy met her gaze. "Yes."

"What if I can't?"

"Let me tell you something Tony doesn't know about Straker," Randy said.

"What?"

"I had entered his woven dreams two other times," Randy admitted. "Like I said, he was the greatest, nicest guy when he was awake. I knew he loved the kids, he took care of the school, and he went to church with his family. But I also knew he was a monster in the dream world. And I realized when Tony sat in my office and told me how he'd progressed, becoming a worse monster in the dreams he weaved, I knew there was only one way to stop him, because I had confronted him twice already." The older man shook his head. "Nothing I did stopped him. You have to understand, when it comes to Nick, it's you or him. The monster in his dreams kills people. It's not Nick. And if you don't stop him, the monster wins. If he wins, he'll kill again and again, because it's what he is. It's what he does. You can't change a viper into a pet turtle. Nick may not be the monster, but Nick feeds the monster." He shrugged. "You're not going to be able to talk him out of killing you. I'm sure all of his other victims have already pleaded with him."

Silence dragged out. Seconds ticked by, and turned into minutes, and then hours. Randy helped himself to her kitchen and made everyone a drink—chamomile tea for Sara and Tony to help them sleep, and strong coffee for himself, to keep him awake.

"Is there anything else we need to do?" Tony asked.

"It would be helpful if you could sleep close together."

"I don't remember you sleeping near my bed all those years ago when I was a kid," Tony pointed out.

Randy grinned. "By then, I didn't need to sleep close to you. I slept in the science lab where he terrorized you. I'd already found my way into the dreams he weaved two other times. This is your first time of trying to find your way there, Tony. You'll find it much easier if you sleep next to her, maybe even hold her hand."

Tony raised an eyebrow to Sara. "Sounds like a plan to me."

A short time later, Sara finished off her tea before she was tucked under her favorite blanket on her bed. With his shoes off, covered with another one of Sara's quilts, Tony stretched out beside her. She couldn't help but notice a connection to him. He needed to maintain a certain closeness to her. And she certainly felt better having him close.

She wished she could stay awake forever and never have to face Nick in a dream again. At the same time, she couldn't fight off the fatigue that overtook her.

Despite the wistfulness that filled her, she still managed a heightened sense of clarity. Nearby Tony snored lightly. She met Randy's gaze. "You put something in our tea, didn't you?"

"A little something, yes, just enough to help you sleep in the right level so, within the dream, you can think clearly and rationally."

"There's no avoiding this, is there?"

Randy shook his head. "I'm afraid not. And I firmly believe you can do what you need to do. Don't get dead, Sara."

Sara laughed, knowing full well there was nothing funny about this situation. "I'll do my best. You're a principal, a super hero for kids with bad dreams, and an anesthesiologist. What else can you do? Can you fix my leaking bathroom sink?"

He gave her a soft smile that she thought was genuine in the candlelight from the candles she'd brought into the bedroom from the hearth. "We'll check it out tomorrow. Now, listen carefully. When you succeed at what you need to do, you need to get to Tony as fast as you can and take his hand. You can't let go of his hand. Do you understand?"

"Take his hand..." she repeated, feeling as if she floated. Tony had fallen asleep holding her hand as Randy had instructed. Now she gave his relaxed hand a squeeze.

"Now go do what you need to do."

It was the last thing she remembered before she awakened in the dream room. She stood near the hearth. There were real flames there.

For a long moment, terror seized all her muscles, making any movement, even breathing, impossible. Sara closed her eyes and listened to the sound of the rain pinging against the window. The heat from the fire in the hearth touched her face. The room smelled of woodsmoke, but brought little comfort.

She changed her mind. She didn't want to do this, didn't want any part of it. After a deep, cleansing breath, she reached out and pinched her arm hard enough that tomorrow, if she survived, she would have a bruise. It didn't wake her up.

"Well, hello, Sara. I've been waiting for you. Don't try to wake yourself up. It won't work this time."

She opened her eyes to find Nick sitting in the red velvet chair.

Dream or no dream, her heart pounded in her chest.

He offered a grin that caused her breath to catch. "You've been trying to avoid me by not sleeping. How long did you think that would last?"

She forced herself to face him, despite the shaking of her knees. At least he hadn't said anything about Tony, so maybe she'd be lucky enough he didn't know she had Tony and Randy on her side. "Obviously not long enough."

He stood and rushed her so quickly, she barely had time to react. One moment, he was across the small room, the next moment he held her by her upper arms and pressed her against the wall near the hearth. "Why did you have to go and make this so hard?"

Did he expect her to make this easy for him? Did he really expect her to just sit back and allow him to kill her without a fight? Had the others done that?

As before, she reacted without thinking and brought her knee into his groin with as much force as she could muster in the tight space between them.

This might be a dream where he had control and could make things appear and happen, but he couldn't make the pain of her action disappear. He let out a heavy gasp and doubled over, letting go of her arms.

She kneed him a second time. With him doubled over, her knee touched up somewhere mid belly. He let out another gasp that sounded more like an "Oooph!"

Sara ran away from him. She knew there was nowhere for her to go, but having him pressing up against her with his stinking breath on her face where he could choke the life out of her simply wasn't an option. She ran to the door she thought of as the door to nowhere, since it would lead to the back side of her bookshelf. The crystal knob was slick and smooth in her grasp, but it refused to budge.

Nick grabbed her from behind and slung her away from the door. She crashed into the red velvet chair, toppled over it, and landed hard enough on the carpet to knock the wind out of her.

Why had she thought she could beat him?

He might be a lanky wimp in the bookstore. Here, in this dream room, he obviously dreamed himself to be strong and fast. She bet he could fly, too, if he dreamed it.

Where was Tony?

Before she could get her breath or her bearings, Nick was on top of her, straddling her chest, making breathing difficult. "I didn't really want it to be like this," he said, putting his hands around her throat. "Why do you pretty women have to make me hurt you? It's as if you can't accept your death unless I hurt you first."

He asked as if he thought this was her fault, as if she was making him kill people, as if she wanted him to kill her.

He spoke as if this was a game to him.

Maybe it was.

Black spots floated in her vision. Strange, she thought, given this was a dream.

His words, his actions made her wonder something else, even as she fought for her life. This was his dream weaving. Why couldn't he just dream her dead? Why did he have to put his hands on her throat in order for him to kill her when all he had to do was dream lit candles on the hearth or rain outside the window? Maybe he wasn't as in control as she thought he was, or better yet, as much as *he* thought he was.

She grasped his thumbs and pulled.

Where the thumb goes, the rest of the hand has no choice but to follow.

He seemed surprised by her actions, that she could do anything to him. His weight still crushed her chest, and she couldn't squirm out from under him even though he struggled against the pull of his thumbs.

Then he was off of her completely.

While she gasped for air and her focus returned, she saw Tony. Her heart did a little flutter of relief. Even when Tony got in one great punch, and the small room filled with the sound of Tony's fist colliding with Nick's face, she knew damned well this wasn't over, not by a long shot.

But she liked the fear she heard in Nick's voice. "You! How could you be here? This is my dream making."

His words were cut off with another punch.

And a terrible realization came to her with Nick's admission of dream making. If Nick made this dream and put her into it, then, if something happened to him, would she be stuck in this little dream room forever? That must be why Randy told her she needed to hold Tony's hand, no matter what.

Before she could voice that worry, Tony appeared to fly across the room and slam into the fake door. A loud groan escaped him, along with the air in his lungs.

Nick clambered to his feet, rubbing his jaw. "This is my dream. And if I want to dream you glued to the door, where you can have a front-row seat while I enjoy choking the life out of Sara, then that's what it'll be! You fucking cop. They're going to find you dead tomorrow, just like Sara. And just like they'll find Tiffany in a few days. She's a sweet redhead I touched yesterday. She's destined be the next woman of my dreams. Better yet, just for grins and groans, I think they'll find you in a coma while I'll keep you here caught in this dream world. I think I'll enjoy dreaming into this dream every person you know and love and killing them slowly in front of you, *Detective Grayson*! But for right now, enjoy the Sara show."

Seeing Tony slam against the door sent all Sara's worries up in smoke. She had to do something now, and she didn't care if she might be stuck there forever. She couldn't let Nick hurt Tony or anyone else.

Tony had told her he hid something in the room. The only hiding place in the entire tiny room was under the red chair.

"I think I'll even kill her and then unglue you for a few minutes so you can feel the full impact of not being able to do a single thing to help her. Or anyone. Without her or you, I'll be free to kill every night."

While Nick boasted his abilities, Sara reached under the chair and grasped what was under there. Even though it was two-and-a-half feet long, she recognized it was a sewing needle. It wasn't unusually heavy, and she could grasp it in one hand despite its length.

Focused on Tony, Nick rattled on about how great he was and how many people he was going to get away with killing. Sara thought he should dream himself a podium to stand behind. She also knew without a shadow of doubt there was only one way to stop this monster.

"Nick?" Sara said softly, drawing his attention as he told Tony he planned to eat Sara's heart.

"What do you want? You should be enjoying the last seconds you have to breathe, Sara." Nick turned to her, his expression feral.

Sara knew if she hesitated, she wouldn't get another chance. She didn't know if he could dream away the huge sewing needle. But she knew he could glue her to the wall as he glued Tony to the door where she could do nothing while he killed her.

It amazed her how easily the sharp needle slid through his clothes and into his chest. Even though he could touch and be touched, the needle the size of a spear pierced through him with the ease of threading through a piece of burlap. Perhaps it was because he was really just a dream figment. Perhaps the boogeyman wasn't that hard to kill, after all.

"I wonder what the true crime author, Simon Dare, would think of your story, Nick."

In the surprise on Nick's face, Sara saw a mixture of shock, hatred, disbelief, and utter horror, all wrapped up in an expression she knew would haunt her dreams for the rest of her life.

Then, as if Randy spoke from the huge living room beyond the open end of the book room, Sara heard, "Take Tony's hand."

Nick fell to his knees and managed to grab her leg. She almost went down with him, but kept her balance as she pulled out of his grasp.

"Bitch," Nick choked out. He sounded as she thought his victims must have sounded as they pleaded for their lives.

She turned to race to Tony and found her legs heavy. If she didn't know better, she'd think she attempted to run through something equivalent to gel or knee-deep, thick mud or drying cement. She glanced down at Nick, found his eyes glazed and unseeing. He was dying or dead, and she'd been right. With Nick unable to end the dream, she and Tony needed to escape. Now.

No longer caught in Nick's grip against the wall, Tony dropped heavily to his knees, catching himself with his palms before his nose hit the carpet.

Black spots again danced before her eyes. Sara's feet were bare, but she felt as if she wore shoes made of cement and a vice squeezed her chest, making breathing harder than when Nick sat on her.

With every ounce of energy she had, she took a chance and leapt toward Tony. She didn't see him take her hand, but she felt it and relaxed against the feel of his touch as he laced his fingers through hers.

Then all went dark, and the miniature dream room faded to black.

Sara woke, groggy. The hung-over, heavy-head feeling that kept her pressed to the pillow took her right back to her college days.

"How do you feel?"

Tony's words were a little loud and all but rang in the space between her ears.

"Drinking all night with my dormmates didn't even leave me feeling this bad," she groaned. "I think I've been run over by a truck."

"Here, start with this."

The bed shifted as Tony sat down on the edge of it next to her. What hit her nose smelled like heaven in a mug. And tasted even better when she took a sip. "You make perfect coffee."

"Thanks. I've had years of practice, and years of being forced to drink sludge, so I definitely know the difference."

She settled into a sitting position braced against the headboard and enjoyed more coffee. "I'm glad you do. Where's Randy?"

"He went to work hours ago."

He smiled. "What time is it?"

"After one in the afternoon."

"What?"

"Randy said you'd need to sleep for a while, probably because you needed to catch up on all the sleep that prick stole from you. I'd make you breakfast, but you don't seem to have any food in this place. So, I thought after you take a shower, we could go to Lizzy's coffee shop and I'll treat you to breakfast." Tony got up and walked to the door of her room.

"Oh, Lizzy has those wonderful cookies. That sounds delicious." Sara swung her legs over the side of the bed, putting the almost-empty cup down on the nightstand.

"Lizzy also makes the best cinnamon rolls. But then, Lizzy makes the best everything when it comes to coffee and pastry."

"Let me take a shower. I'll do my best to keep it under ten minutes."

"I'll be waiting." The door closed behind him.

One Month Later

The morning illustrated spring was in full force. Birds sang and chirped. The sun peeked from behind the horizon. The breeze was refreshing.

Again, Tony had his shoes off. He rocked back in one of two rockers Sara moved from her porch to the small covered balcony of his house. His renovations were moving along well, and now included Sara's input. Sara, also barefoot, but dressed in jeans and one of Tony's oversized shirts, relaxed in the other rocker as the two of them enjoyed watching the town of Mossy Point wake up with the sunrise. The breakfast board he'd prepared for them was on the small table between them. She enjoyed a sausage link as she sipped her coffee.

"It's been a month," he commented. "How are you sleeping?"

"You should know. You've slept beside me and held my hand ever since."

She didn't point out ever since *what.*

Yes, he'd slept beside her ever since. Yes, he held her hand as they fell asleep together. It seemed like the most natural thing in the world to do, and he knew without a shadow of a doubt he couldn't and wouldn't sleep at all without her beside him. Neither of them questioned it. But he wondered if the dream they shared somehow connected them. Not that it mattered. Now that he had her in his life, he found he needed her more than his next breath.

"Are you asking because you don't want to sleep with me anymore?" she asked. "Are you saying it's time I move back to my own bed alone, because if that's the case, these chairs go with me."

Tony shook his head, smiling. "No, I'm not saying that at all. I'm asking because I don't want to keep going between your house and mine. I know it's fast, and I know we've only really known each other for little more than a month, but I want to be with you. And not just at night. But I need to know how you feel, especially since I got some information yesterday."

"What kind of information?" she asked.

"Nick's autopsy came back."

"Oh? Don't tell me, the medical examiner found a needle in his heart?"

He let out a chuckle and took a sip of his coffee. "Yeah, weird, isn't it? The ME thinks, since there was no evident trace of it piercing through his skin, he must have swallowed it, and it went through his esophagus where it could pierce his heart."

"I always thought there was something strange about that guy."

Tony was comforted by the idea she was able to talk about Nick and not be emotional or affected. He couldn't help but wonder if sleeping together as they were was what helped them to heal and move beyond the horrific experience. "Me, too."

She eyed him over the rim of her cup. "Was there anything else?"

"Yes, it appears he had traces of odd activity in his brain."

That got her attention. "Odd activity?"

"The ME wonders if he had seizures as a kid or something." Tony leaned forward to snag a pastry while she digested that bit of information.

"His ability to weave dreams could be seen in his brain?"

"I don't know," he said around a mouthful. "I guess anything's possible."

"Can I have that upper smaller bedroom to set up my equipment for my podcast?" Sara asked.

"Are you sure you don't want the bigger one?"

"Smaller is better," Sara said cheerfully. "Sound is better with less echoing."

"Are you sure you want to move in with me?"

"Are you sure you want to hold my hand every night?"

Tony took a deep breath. "I want to hold your hand every night, and then some."

"When can I move in?"

"Whenever it works out for you," he replied. "As long as you're here to hold my hand before I go to sleep." He took another bite and after chewing, he asked, "And where should we put that little dream room."

"Oh," Sara said, with a smile, "I already took care of that."

Small Town Urban Legend

"Did it ever occur to you that this all might be some sort of a hoax? Like a story to scare people and keep them out of this place? I mean, after all, I'm not sure I believe a ten-year-old little girl can manage to kill her father, the nanny, the cook, and the housekeeper, just before dinner, all in a single night. Really?" Conner asked as he and his four friends stood in the dark foyer of Devlin Mansion.

The musty, stale scent of unuse hung in the air like the unchanging smell of a boys' high school locker room.

"I'm telling you, Connor, that is the legend," argued Jax. "The entire household was murdered by the little girl. And today is the hundred and fiftieth anniversary of those murders. The moon is in its dark phase, just as it was then. The date alone will make this an awesome party. It will be a perfect ending to the week of hazing. We can stay the entire night in Dansville Manor. And everyone will have a great story tomorrow for Family Sunday. Maybe we might find answers as to what really happened, but I understand one of the victims was actually hanged from that rope right up there."

Jax shined his flashlight up to the second story loft-landing. There was a rope tied to the fourth rail rung just before the stairs started down their curved descent. The rope, complete with a noose tied on the dangling end, hung down perhaps five feet.

Conner stared.

Raven, Avery, and Jason stared, too.

Jax felt like bursting as he fought to keep from laughing. Since he had their undivided attention, he continued with his ghost story. "The true legend is the little girl killed everyone one by one with an ax. Supposedly, the nanny went to find the child and never returned. So, the father searched for the daughter and her nanny. One by one as each victim was alone, the ten-year-old girl hacked them to pieces. Then the girl was the one who hung herself over the railing. I did extensive research on this." Jax didn't add that in all his research, he was unable to find what actually became of little Charlotte Danville.

But Jax liked the idea of a rope hanging from the loft. Even more, he liked the reactions of his so-called friends as they stared at it. He found scaring these four people empowering.

"Wait a minute," Jason said. "I know this takes me back to my Eagle Scout days, but that's a timber hitch."

"What's a timber hitch?" Avery asked.

Jax couldn't help but notice Avery held Jason's hand. He guessed those two were on their way to being an item. He had the feeling it was going to be short lived, but too bad, so sad. Avery looked a bit pale in the glow of the flashlight Jax held. Good, he wanted her scared.

He wanted her to be scared. A lot.

He'd had other ideas for Avery. He even got his hands on some knock out drops to use on her while he took a few pictures. But then the idea of Devlin Mansion came to him, and it was like killing four birds with one stone. And although he would still love to take a few pictures, he couldn't chance having a single shred of evidence on his phone.

"It's a type of knot. And see, most people wouldn't know the best knot to tie. But you're trying tell us that a ten-year-old little girl knew how to tie that knot, then managed to hang herself over that rail? I say we get the heck out of here and do something else. There's a great party at Tri Signa Delta, and we are missing it."

"Oh, come on," Jax coaxed, "I told you we are going to have a fantastic party here. Here's what I thought we could do—check this place out, have a party to remember, one that will create a legend of its own. We could even invite all the other frats and sororities. Then next month, we could have a Halloween party here. I mean what better venue for a fun party than a real haunted house. I already told a bunch of people to be here at ten. That gives us two hours to move some furniture around, set up some food, and find the right place for a keg.

Like on that table over there," he paused and shined his light to a nearby table, "I've got candles and chips and some drinks. I have three other frat guys bringing the keg. I need you guys to help out just a little bit, if you don't mind. Of course, if you'd rather go back to Tri Signa Delta, go ahead, but by the sound of it, most of them plan to come over here. Suit yourselves."

Jax walked away, heading to the table where he'd shined his light. He struck a match and lit two of the candles he'd placed there. The two candles gave off a softer glow than the LED light of his flashlight. Somehow, the two small flickering flames still managed to light up the entire room, revealing the cobwebs, the dusty black and white checker-board tiled floor, and the ornate staircase that curved around to the lofted balcony of the second floor. The carved lion on the newel post stared at them. There was now enough light to see the wooden lion heads that were carved into the backs of the double front doors.

Of the four of his friends, Jax certainly hoped there would be one who wouldn't go running off like a scared rabbit, who had enough strength and willpower to keep the others there to play his game. If not, he'd have to think of something else.

But then one of them did have the courage. That one turned out to be Raven when she ventured further into the foyer. "Look at that!" She looked up and the others all followed suit.

Above their heads hung a round chandelier made up of what looked to be a hundred candles.

Although Raven wasn't the person he would have guessed would have wanted to stay inside of the walls of Devlin Mansion, he was pleasantly surprised. He drew closer to her and looked up, too. "It's so cool, isn't it? And look over there." Jax motioned to the far wall. "It's the rope they used to lower it down and light that monstrosity. I had planned to light it and have the place lit up when you guys got here, but I have no idea how heavy it might be. I thought it best to wait until you guys could help me. I figured we could carefully untie it, lower it to the floor, light maybe every other candle, pull it back up, and have the place lit up before everyone else gets here."

"You aren't serious about lighting that thing up, are you?" Jason asked.

"Sure am," Jax replied. "That way, we aren't wandering around in the dark. Especially since you all are a bunch of pussies being afraid of the dark."

"And what if it burns the place down?" Jason sounded more afraid than Avery looked.

Jax looked at Jason and said nothing for a long moment. He didn't understand why Jason was suddenly the party pooper. He wasn't the party pooper when it came to making a laughing stock out of Jax. A week ago, Jason had stolen Jax's clothes and towel when Jax had been in the shower. The frat house was quiet and even dark. Jax had thought everyone was out. When he made his way from the bathroom to his room soaking wet and naked, Jason suddenly flipped on the lights, revealing the party of people there watching, and then laughing, while Jax streaked to his room. If Jason had played such 'jokes' on everyone, Jax probably would have been able to laugh it off. But Jason seemed to always make Jax the butt of his jokes and pranks.

"The place is not going to burn down," Jax insisted.

"Oh, come on. We can be careful. Besides it's not going to burn the place down," Raven reiterated. "It was obviously used for eons and never burned anything but the candles."

Her words were enough to get the others to stay. Jax could have hugged her, but he knew without a doubt his hugging her would probably scare her away faster than anything creepy in the house. He met her gaze through the candlelight. "It's going to be such a fun party."

He looked at his phone, checking the time. "We have less than two hours until all the other frat guys get here. I brought some snacks, some chips and dip, some paper plates and stuff, and, of course, the famous red plastic cups."

"I only see one little table here with your stuff on it, Jax." Conner argued.

Jax didn't laugh, but thought it was funny—get the guys out of the frat house and into unfamiliar territory where they didn't have safety in numbers and an audience to laugh at their nasty jokes, and they were just a couple of cowards with excuses.

"Yeah, well, you know what, Conner? I doubt anyone's going to stop us if we remove the white sheets, rearrange the furniture, and use it. Are you game? Or are you going to be a little scaredy cat, running home to mommy with your tail tucked between your legs, held there by your itty-bitty balls?"

Jax knew his words may cause a fight. Just last week, during a drunken game of truth or dare, Conner had revealed that until the age of twelve, he'd slept with a flashlight because he was afraid of the dark. He didn't like scary movies, he shied away from anything that might remotely be creepy.

When Conner looked as though he might bolt through those doors with the lions on them, Jax went on, "All I'm asking is that you just help me set up for the party. If you don't want to stay after that, fine with me. I've already been through every room of this house today, and all I've found is dust and spiders and cobwebs. I've got a couple of prank things to hide in closets and even some of those motion activated things that do evil laughing when someone walks by. I was thinking we could put those on the stairs, and then we'd know who might be trying to sneak up to one of the six bedrooms up there to screw around."

Of course, he said nothing of the traps he set upstairs that took him all day. When his fellow party-goers still appeared skeptical, he continued, "I don't know if the legend holds true, and I don't really care. I just think this will make for a great party, and I hope you guys will help me set up for it. And if it's a success, I was thinking in another month and a half or so at the end of October, near Halloween, we could make it a haunted house fundraiser for the frat."

Jax looked at each of them, giving them all an imploring expression. He thought he might change his major to acting.

"I'm in," said Raven. "I think it sounds like a fun party. I'll be glad to help you set up some drinks and snacks. I could even jump out and make somebody scream!"

Jax could have kissed her, he really could. But then she went over to Conner and laced her long, delicate fingers through Conner's. Her blood-red nails shined in the dim lighting of their flashlights and the candle light.

"Do you want to be one of the couples who tries to sneak up the stairs?" Conner's words were whispered, but Jax heard them.

Raven shrugged, "We'll see."

Jax sucked in a deep breath, working to keep from upchucking, working to keep his rage in check. He liked Raven. She could be nice. Conner, however, had a few lessons to learn. Jax didn't give any of them time to back out. He went over to the table, pulled out the big plastic bag of still-in-their packages decorated paper plates and napkins. He wanted this party to be perfect. So, it hadn't bothered him in the least when he spent his entire meager paycheck on snacks and paper products that only these four party-goers were going to enjoy.

The chandelier was not nearly as heavy as it appeared, and the three young men easily untied the knot in the rope and lowered it to the floor. The pulley at the ceiling that held it gave barely an aged creak.

Raven had a lighter and made use of it, counting the candles as she walked the circle and lit each one. They totaled eighty-nine. She also thought far enough ahead to make certain each old wax candle was seated safely, and no lit candle would come falling down as they, once again, carefully raised it up near the ceiling.

"I don't think we should be doing this," Conner argued as he and Jason held the rope and Jax retied the knot that held the chandelier in its rightful position. "I don't think we should be in this house at all.

There's a really heavy feeling here. Despite all the light from that thing." He looked upward at the humungous candelabra.

Jax followed his gaze and looked up before looking around. The glow of the candles filled with room with soft, welcoming light that was so warm the cobwebs sparkled in it. "You know, Conner, I never took you for a chicken. But how about this? I promise we'll put everything back just the way we found it. Even the candles up there." He pointed to the chandelier, "If any of those candles burn down to the hub, I'll come back and replace them, leaving it even better than the way we found it, how's that?"

Conner seemed to study the chandelier for a moment. "Whatever."

No one else commented about not being in the house.

Raven continued to look up. "Wow, that's cool."

Then one by one, they began to draw in the courage to wander away from the main large room.

Jason opened packages of paper plates before he and Avery went into the next room, which was a dusty sitting area. Jax remembered studying this room looking for potential places for his traps and found nothing but dust filled furniture. There was no way he would even consider sitting on one of the three sofas in there. He said nothing as Jason and Avery lit a few more candles and half dragged, half carried a table closer to the foyer.

Avery pulled the what-used-to-be white sheet that now appeared gray from the table. In the candle light, dust flew like glitter in a snow globe after being shook up. She coughed and muttered, "I should probably use my inhaler."

Jax heard Raven whisper something to Conner about checking out other rooms to look for good places to hide to scare people when they arrived. Within ten minutes, he was alone in the foyer. He quietly slipped out the front door to make sure his night would be complete.

Wind whistled through the eaves of the house. Dry leaves of late summer crackled in the nearby woods. The full moon was high. Jax thought he heard something in the nearby trees. Was it a foot step snapping twigs? Or just the night settling in? He looked around and saw nothing more beyond what he'd seen when he investigated the house earlier. There was just the overgrown walk and remnants of a fence along with part of a gate. Moonlight shined on the porch, sending shadows dancing with the branches of nearby trees that moved with the night breeze.

An owl hooted somewhere nearby. The smell of a mixture of dust, rot, mold, and wood touched him like cold fingertips.

Subtly, he leaned down and peered into a nearby cracked window pane. He saw Avery and Jason disappear up the stairs. Raven and Conner moved opposite the kitchen. None of them noticed his absence.

He took care of business outside, making certain no one would have the opportunity for a fast departure. Then, as stealthy as he'd left, he returned to the foyer of Devlin Mansion. For a long moment, he stood and listened, deciding where to start first. Then he slipped his hooded cape over his head. His plan was to listen. If his four friends didn't fall into the traps he set for them, he planned to scare them into his traps.

When he'd been in the house previously, he'd found what he thought was a perfect hiding place—a small, hidden compartment in the wall beyond the door leading down to the cellar beneath the main stairs.

He hadn't, however, taken into account that, while the small space accommodated him sitting with his knees tucked to his chin, there was not room for the ax prop he planned to use to scare the others. He was forced to leave it propped in a nearby corner before he climbed into the tight space. Although he hadn't put it on yet, he did take with him the rubber mask he'd bought for this occasion. The mask was that of a doll face. It wasn't by any means a scary mask, compared to something of a werewolf or something ghoulish. It was the closest he could find of a little girl, as his plan was to scare the others mimicking the legendary child who killed her entire family.

He had barely managed to fold himself into his tight hiding place when he heard noise from upstairs. He recognized a muffled scream from Avery. He heard Jason's yell, "What kind of game are you playing now, Avery?"

In the dark, Jax smiled. His plan was taking shape. The traps he'd set would all work. All he had to do was settle in and be patient.

Upstairs, Avery and Jason moved down the hall. Avery carried a single lit candle to light their way.

"I think I changed my mind. It's creepy up here. I think the dust is thicker. Downstairs in the candle light is better," Avery said. "I should go find my bag and use my inhaler."

"Too late to change your mind." Jason opened the door to the first bedroom.

"Wait," Avery tugged back on her hand Jason held.

"What now, Ave? Every time we get the opportunity to be alone for a while, you tell me to wait. What's your problem?"

"I think if we're going to do anything, we should do it in the last bedroom."

"*If* we're going to do anything?" He leaned down, quick as a snake striking, and kissed her hard, forcing his tongue into her mouth. "I thought you wanted this as much as I did. Now, you're saying, 'if.' And why in hell would I wait for the last bedroom, when it looks as if there's a perfectly good one right here?"

"If anyone comes looking for us, we'd have more time to hear them approaching from down the hall. I don't know if you noticed, but this floor so far has creaked with every step we've taken. I feel like the floor shifts as we walk down the hall. Besides, give me five minutes to..." To what? She fought to find the right words because she suddenly wasn't so sure she wanted to have any skin-to-skin relationship with him. In the last week, she discovered him to be nothing more than pushy.

"I'll give you three out here in the dark hallway; but that's it. And when I step into the room with you, you'd better be naked, wet, and ready for the best fuck you've ever had."

Avery had heard a lot of rumors about Jason, and before now, she'd thought him charming. But now following his last sentence, she wondered just how many of the rumors were true. In one statement, she discovered just how conceited and demanding and impatient he was. She stood in the hall staring at him, trying to read him, as she did a mental debate about which direction to take. Obviously, she stood for a few seconds too long because he grabbed her about her throat with his left hand and pressed her against the wall.

The action caused hot wax from the candle she held to spill over onto her fingers, burning her.

"Don't you even think about dropping that candle." His tone was low and more frightening than the idea of the haunted house around her. "You aren't thinking about changing your mind again, are you, Avery? Because you'd better not be. I'm tired of waiting. And I'm tired of you teasing me."

"No," she said. "I just needed a little time."

"Well, you had three minutes, but now I think we're down to two. I'll be out here, counting down the seconds. Now, get moving, time's wasting."

He let her go.

With the trembles that coursed through her, more hot wax covered that which was already dried on her hand as she quicky made her way down the hall.

She stepped inside the last bedroom on the left, closed the door behind her and leaned against it, forcing her breaths to calm. Then she turned and investigated the door more in the light of her candle to see if she could lock it. There was a skeleton keyhole, but, of course, she had no key.

She leaned her forehead against the door and closed her eyes, relishing in the cool smoothness of it as she forced her breaths and her heart to calm while she contemplated what to do. Any minute he was going to come barging in, expecting her to feed his over-inflated ego and libido. She needed to search for a way out of here. She faced the room again, determined to find, at the very least, a hiding place.

A slight scream escaped her before a man's hand clasped over her mouth, cutting off further sound. She dropped the candle. The room was cast into utter darkness as the tiny flame was extinguished.

The man in the room was tall and dressed in dark clothes. Even his face looked black. Before she could force any movement through the terror that froze her muscles, he flipped on a flashlight. It was so bright the suddenness of it temporarily blinded her. He shined the light up under his chin, showing her his face was striped with black grease paint like special ops guys on TV. He placed a single finger across his lips, asking her to stay quiet.

His gaze shifted from her to the door as she heard Jason in the hallway. "What kind of game are you playing now, Avery?"

"My name is Tony, Detective Tony Grayson. I'm a cop with the Mossy Point Police Department," the stranger whispered. "Can I trust you to stay quiet?"

She nodded, and the stranger who called himself a cop let go of her mouth. She worked again to catch her breath as she stared at him. She was certain her heart pounded in her throat. He pointed his flashlight to his other hand, in which he held a police badge. The badge was silver and shaped like a small shield. The reflection of the flashlight momentarily blinded her, and she was forced to blink several times before she could, again, focus on the shadows of Detective Tony Grayson's face.

"Avery?" came a call from the hall.

"Tell him you dropped your candle."

"I just dropped my candle," she called out.

"One minute," Jason called back to her.

"He's brought you here to kill you." Detective Tony Grayson slipped the badge into his pocket.

From the hall came Jason's call again. "Forty-five seconds."

"Jason?" Avery asked.

"No," the cop replied. "Jax."

"What?"

With Jason still counting down the second from the hall, the cop shined his flashlight toward the far end of the room, revealing a large, jagged black area in the floor.

"Is that a hole in the floor, Detective Grayson?" She suddenly felt as if there was an equally big hole in her chest, and she couldn't breathe.

"Call me Tony."

"Is the floor rotten, should we go downstairs?" Her questioning words come out in a rush. She didn't wait for Tony to answer. "If I hadn't stopped to lean against the door, if I had rushed in here..."

"You would have fallen clear through to the earthen floor of the cellar. I put an old mattress down there, but I'm not certain how much it would help a two-story fall. And no, the floor isn't rotten. He had to get his hands on a big-ass power saw to cut that hole as well as the one below it in the kitchen."

"How do you know this?" The desperation that coursed through her caused her words to tremble.

"That's not important. What is important is that I get you and Jason and Raven and Conner out of here. Alive."

From right outside the door, "Avery, time's up. You better be ready." The door knob rattled and turned.

"Jason's expecting—"

The cop turned off his flashlight. "I know what he's expecting. And he's going to have to wait."

"Probably forever when it comes to me."

"That's good thinking. From what I know about Jason, you deserve better." With a smooth gentleness Avery found endearing and unexpected, Grayson placed his hands on her upper arms and slid her away from the door. He pulled open the door, apparently just as Jason pushed it inward.

Jason fell into the room, maintaining his balance because he still held the door knob.

Avery's eyes were accustomed enough to the dark to see his expression of shock. For some odd reason, the sight brought about a giggle that threatened to boil forth from her lips.

"What the—" was all Jason managed to get out before—and with not so much gentleness as when he grabbed Avery—the cop grabbed him by his shirt and dragged him into the room and pressed him against the wall in nearly the same fashion as Jason had held her moments ago.

"Shut your mouth. Don't say a word."

Jason's shock wore off and he was back to being the tough guy he saw himself to be. "Yeah? Who the fuck are you, and why the fuck should I listen to you?"

Avery's whisper of, "He's a cop," was lost in another shocking move as Tony slapped Jason across the face. The momentum of that strike sent Jason turning to his right. Tony finished out the action, grabbing Jason by his arm. He shoved Jason, while twisting his arm behind his back until Jason turned completely around. He pressed Jason against the door.

"Now, you listen to me, you little prick. I'm Detective Tony Grayson, with the Mossy Point Police Department. I'm here to save your ass. There's not a lot of time, and I don't want to spend what little there is fighting with the likes of you. Your buddy, Jax, downstairs has the entire house rigged with traps designed to kill you and your friends. Now, if you don't want to listen to me or do what I say, feel free to slide down the banister and see how long you last. Truth be told, I don't much care. I don't like you. I don't like how you treat women. And I can always write in my report that I advised you, and you ignored me. I'm going to let you go, and I know you gave Avery a whomping three whole minutes to get ready for you. Well, I'm only giving you ten seconds to decide how this is going to work."

Tony let him go suddenly. Jason slid half way down the door before he managed to gain his balance. Jason turned around, his eyes wide and filled with nothing short of fury. His panting breaths were loud in the silence, and Avery again fought back a giggle at the way his nostrils flared like a bull ready to charge.

"Are you in or out?" Tony asked.

"Let me see your badge, Tony."

Tony fished it out of his pocket, and Jason examined it in the light from Tony's flashlight. "You can call me Detective Grayson."

Jason looked at Avery. "Are you okay?" He sounded almost sincere in his concern for her.

"Yeah, I'm fine."

"In or out?" Tony asked again.

"I'm in. And if I find out this is all a lie, I'll fucking kill you."

Tony appeared unaffected by the threat. "And if you do anything that jeopardizes this mission or gets any of your friends hurt, I will let Jax kill you."

"So, show me one of these supposed traps."

A few seconds later, the three of them stood around the hole at the far side of the room. The ground floor of the kitchen was lit by what may have been a candle, but the cellar was dark and looked like an endless tunnel.

"Shit," Jason let out as he stared down.

"Since you know he wants to kill us, do you know why?" Avery asked.

"You stopped going out with Jax to go out with him." Tony pointed to Jason.

A wave of sudden, hot anger barreled through her. "Are you kidding me? He wants to kill me because I stopped dating him?"

"I think so. I don't know all the true reasons. I just know his pretending to be your friend, is just that. Pretending. So, each of you can think about whatever it was you may have done to him. Whatever it was, he thinks it's enough to kill you, and cover it up as accidents in a haunted house while you all are having a party."

As they looked down, Raven came into view in the kitchen. With her arms filled with a box of what was obviously a variety of bags of chips, she didn't see the hole cut into of the floor. And she was just lucky enough to walk past it without falling down it. To Avery, it appeared that three inches to the left, and Raven would have taken a tumble.

Just like that, Tony's hand was over Avery's mouth again, stopping her from calling out to Raven.

"Don't call out, give no warning."

"Why not?" Jason asked.

"I assure you, wherever Jax is hiding, it's a place where he can watch and/or listen to see if you fall into the traps he's created. If you warn anyone, if he knows we're on to him, this could turn into something worse." He let go of Avery.

"How do I know you aren't the one trying to kill us, that you didn't cut this hole in the floor?"

"If I had been the one who cut this hole in the floor and wanted you dead, I assure you, Jason, you'd already be down there on the floor of the cellar."

Avery thought his words made sense.

"So, stay quiet. The two of you are supposed to be up here, not knowing anything about what might be going on anywhere else in the house."

"Even if we were up here screwing around, and we heard someone fall or scream, we'd check it out," Avery argued.

Tony looked at Jason. "I somehow doubt that. We need to get back downstairs. But be careful, there's a trip wire waiting for you."

"Me?" Jason asked.

"That's right."

"How do you know this?"

"I couldn't explain it if I tried. You're going to have to just trust me."

"Maybe we should go back down another way," Jason suggested.

Avery thought Jason looked as scared as he'd made her feel a short time before. Seeing that fear etched into his expression empowered her as nothing else ever had.

"No, we need to go the way Jax would expect you to go. And here's what I need for you to do."

As Avery listened to the cop tell what would work for getting them through the set traps unscathed, she was filled with an odd mixture of awe and fear that set her heart pounding. Why couldn't Jason be a quick-thinking hero like this cop who showed up to save her? Probably because he thought with the wrong head, that's why.

The calming sound of Detective Grayson's voice was like a warm blanket on a cold, blustery day. She didn't care how he knew what Jax had in store her for, she was indeed thankful she hadn't fallen into the dark cellar. Without hesitation, she followed Detective Grayson out the door. Jason lagged by a few seconds.

Fifteen minutes before Jason and Avery met Detective Tony Grayson, Raven Davenport looked about the Devlin Mansion in awe. More than once, she considered finding a way to gain a loan to purchase the property; and all she'd seen of the house so far was the foyer, drawing room, and the scant kitchen. A single lit candle on the table inside the doorway was enough to reveal there were no cabinets in the kitchen. Nor were there any appliances or fixtures. But then, perhaps there may have never been any. There was a closed door at the far dark end which she had no doubt was a pantry. There was a vacant spot where she assumed there'd been some sort of sink. But marks on the wall indicated it had long ago been ripped out.

She'd grown up with a grandfather who ran an antique store, and she had his eye for priceless pieces.

And the—not one, but two—butcher blocks in the kitchen were beyond priceless. As were the tables and one armoire she'd seen. While she'd love to take any one of them home, she also knew they belonged to the house, and it was one thing that made them priceless. Tomorrow, in the light of day, she planned to explore the house more. Then she planned to find out who the present owner might be.

From the table in the foyer, she grabbed another box of snacks. She let out a startled scream as someone poked her ribs and shouted, "Boo!" She dropped the box and the top bag of chips bounced out, landing on the floor, making a lot of noise.

Conner busted out laughing.

"Oh you!" She gave his arm a slap that seemed to echo through the empty living room. "All the chips are probably crushed." She tucked the bag of chips back into the box before picking it back up.

"I doubt anyone's going to care as they look around this place. Can you believe this place?" he said, not put off by scaring her or her slapping him.

"I know, right?"

"The frat guys are going to love this. Do you want to know the creepiest thing?"

"I'm sure you're going to tell me."

"The dining room, over on the other side of the kitchen."

"What about it? I haven't seen it yet," she said.

"It's all set up in there."

"For what? The party?" Raven asked.

"No, more like the family's about to sit down for dinner."

"What?"

He took the box from her. "Here, put this down for a minute and walk around this way, it's closer than heading through the kitchen." Conner took her hand and led her back across the foyer and into what was obviously the dining room on the opposite side of the kitchen.

Raven stared for a long moment. "You did this," she accused him.

"I swear, I didn't. I carried a candle in here to check out this room, and I found it exactly like this."

Raven stepped to the round dining room table. The table cloth was not a white sheet like those which covered most of the rest of the tables they'd seen thus far. At first, she thought the table cloth had flowers on it, but then she pulled out her lighter and lit the candles in the two candelabras that graced the table. The cloth that was revealed in the soft glow was not flower petals but patterned spider webs of a crocheted table cloth. The five China place settings were set in front of chairs in perfect precision, as if preparing for a formal dinner party.

Raven picked up a dinner plate. "China?"

"Looks like it."

"There are five places set, and there are five of us. Do you think the ghosts were expecting us for dinner?"

Conner let out a chuckle that sounded just a bit apprehensive. "Either that, or Jax is up to more than just a scary frat party. Maybe he wanted to make this like a really special dinner."

"I can see him buying a few snacks and red plastic cups, but I can't see him splurging on china or setting the table. I mean, what are we going to do, eat chips and salsa on china?"

"I doubt it. Anyway, he made a really big point about buying red plastic cups, so I think that's about his limit."

Raven chuckled. "You know, this place is so beautiful, filled with antiques like it's somehow been frozen in time. But then, I step into this room. And..." She paused. "I think out of this entire house that I've seen so far, this room is the creepiest. It's colder than a dinosaur frozen in time."

"I agree with you. It still feels so heavy to me."

"Do you think this room is where everyone was murdered?"

Conner shrugged "I wouldn't be surprised."

"And speaking of Jax, do you know where he went? I want to ask him about this." Raven indicated the set table.

"I have no idea. In this house, he could be in one of any of the dozen rooms."

"There are twelve rooms in this house?" Raven asked.

"Well, I haven't exactly counted them, but I wouldn't be surprised," Conner admitted. "And I haven't been upstairs yet."

"Can you blow the candles out. I don't want to have to come back in here. I don't like the feel of this room," she said.

"Do you want to explore the cellar with me?"

Raven laughed. "Yeah, sure, since this room isn't creepy enough. But maybe in a minute. I was going to set up snacks in here, but I've changed my mind. I think I'll keep them all on the tables in the foyer."

"Well, I'll meet you down there, then."

They split ways. Conner headed to the stairs going out one of the dining room doors. Raven headed out the other moving toward the kitchen with the box of snacks again in her arms.

Conner opened the door under the stairs that led to the cellar. It opened with a loud creak. He stepped into the small landing that led down. The door closed on its own behind him, again filling the room with the sounds of rusted, old hinges.

And Raven headed through the kitchen. She rounded past the pantry. At her third step, the floor disappeared beneath her feet.

In the shadows, Jax listened to them go their own ways heading toward traps he carefully set. The party began.

Jax had the perfect hiding place. He couldn't see any of his traps, but he would be able to hear when they were tripped.

The first came within minutes. He heard the splinter of wood giving away. He heard a scream, which came from the direction of where he knew Raven to be. It had to be Raven screaming as she fell from the kitchen to the cellar. Then again, perhaps it was Avery falling all the way through from the upstairs bedroom down through broken floors to the cellar. Either would work out well for him. He thought he heard a dull thud as whoever it was landed on the floor in the cellar. He saw and listened and waited, wishing he'd thought to buy a few cameras so he could have a visual of this night, of his excellent plan, and see exactly who fell through the hole in the floor.

From the tiny stairs leading to the cellar, Jax heard Conner's muffled yell. "Raven! Raven, what happened!" The door leading to the cellar stairs jiggled and rattled as Conner worked the handle and the door refused to open.

Jax had done a brilliant job on the door knob, making sure it opened from the foyer side, but he loosened the handle on the inside stairs side. Once the handle came off, there would be no way to open the door from the inside.

Then Jax heard a thunk and a muffled, "Well, fuck."

Which told Jax the door handle was now completely off and had hit a stair, sealing Conner into the stairwell that led to the cellar. All Conner needed to do was head down the stairs—the missing stairs which he couldn't see were missing in the darkness. Those had been a bear to saw off and had taken Jax hours of work. He'd made sure there was no escape from the cellar.

In his dark little hidey hole, Jax heard Conner let out a few more choice words and, "Where's the damned light?" As if there would be a light. There were no lights at all in this entire house. Did Conner just forget all the candles that took Raven ten minutes to light? Jax smiled. He supposed Conner could turn on the flashlight on his cell phone. The question was: would he turn it on before moving down the stairs?

Then Jax heard something close to a yelp coming from Conner in the cellar stairwell and thought guess not.

At this rate, his so-called friends would soon be done, all trapped in the cellar. This was going much faster than he anticipated.

Now he just had to wait for Avery and Jason to finish upstairs. If the rumors were true, it shouldn't take more than five minutes.

In the dark, musty, stillness, Jax waited. Tomorrow–if he needed to wait that long—after he crawled from the house, called for help and told everyone how hard he tried—but was unsuccessful—to help his friends, how the ghosts killed them and claimed more souls for the house, he'd be a legend. No, he'd be an urban legend.

He saw himself being on talk shows and newscasts. Of course, he would give them a good show, with real tears and words of regret about how much he missed his friends and how sorry he was he couldn't save them. Without Jason around and taking the spotlight as he always did, Jax would be seen as the handsome hero. Women would flock to him.

Maybe he should leave his secret hiding place and search out Avery and Jason, see exactly where they are.

He moved slightly.

The sounds of a child giggling stopped him.

The laughter came from right outside the small cabinet door where Jax hid.

Then there came high pitched words, spoken as if the child was attempting to whisper, but didn't quite know how. "Ollie, Ollie, Oxen Free! Come out! Come out! Wherever you are!"

Jax had been all over this house today, in every single room. There had not been any sign of a kid anywhere. As a matter of fact, the only evidence there had ever been a child in the house was in one of the upstairs bedrooms where there were still dusty dolls that stared at you when you entered the room and a dollhouse that was a small replica of this house. The dollhouse was as scary as the real house because the first time he noticed it, the five dolls within it were all in the foyer. The second time he went into that room after cutting the hole in the floor of the bedroom at the end of the hall, the dolls were in various places as if someone had moved them. One doll was in the cellar, one was in the kitchen, one was sitting on the stairs, and two others were in the upstairs bedroom at the end of the hall.

Then another sound drew his attention.

"Hey, Avery." It was Jason speaking, sounding close, coming from the direction of the stairs. "Where'd you—" His muffled question was cut off by the thumping sounds of him tumbling down the stairs. He obviously reached Jax's trip wire.

Awesome.

Dare he venture out to take a peek, see how the tumble affected Jason?

There was another child's giggle, but now it sounded further away.

Jax opened the cabinet door, just enough to look out with one eye.

In his line of vision, he saw the bottom of the stairs and what was obviously Jason's hand resting on the floor. He would not be able to see the entire picture unless he opened the cabinet fully and stuck his head out.

He heard motion—footsteps approaching, so he quickly closed himself back into the small space of the cabinet.

"Jason? Jason!" It was Avery, obviously following Jason from upstairs. She let out a scream, apparently seeing him at the bottom of the stairs. Then another scream mixed in with the snap of wood splintering.

He could only guess Avery, in her haste to reach Jason, managed to find the sawed-out rungs of the railing. There was even a slap as he could only assume she fell through the cut rail rungs and landed on the tiled floor.

That should be everyone!

Now, he'd climb out and see, finish off whoever needed finishing off.

They were all such good friends. He chuckled out loud at his own sarcastic thought and envisioned how he'd be comforted at their funerals. He would tell the cops it was Jason's idea to have a party at the haunted Devlin Mansion. He would cry real tears when he reported how he'd told everyone it was an old, old house, they needed to be extra careful.

He unfolded himself from the small cabinet space, grunting softly as he stretched out his stiff joints after sitting so long in the tight place.

He looked over at the tile at the bottom of the stairs. Jason lay there, unmoving, a pool of red spreading out on the floor where his face met the tile. For a moment, Jax considered using his ax and giving Jason a few whacks. After all, Jason deserved it. The shower prank wasn't the only nasty trick Jason had ever played on him. In the end, Jax didn't reach for the ax. He still might, later, but not at this moment.

Not far away, Avery lay on the floor also, obviously after falling from the loft above. She lay on her belly, her face turned away from him, but there was a pool of red beneath her face.

He had no doubt Conner and Raven were also now lying on the earthen floor of the cellar.

Jax pulled his phone. The time was a quarter past nine.

Just how long should he wait before calling the police. He knew from watching TV the cops always paid attention to the time the 9-1-1 call was made. And did he really need to feign his own injury?

He probably should. He needed to make this night as believable as possible. Besides an injury would add to the empathy and attention. He thought about the ax and worked to devise a way to get an ax injury. That would make the best ghost story. After all, the little girl killed her family with an ax. What a legend that would be! Ghost of child ax murderer still killing people in haunted house!

And Jax would be at the center of that legend.

Then the plan came to him. He would slice open his leg with the ax, wipe off his fingerprints, leave the ax inside, crawl out the door, and call 9-1-1 from the porch. He would tell the police he crawled away from the ghost of a little girl, that it appeared she couldn't leave the house, which was a good thing since he could go no further than the porch before he became too weak.

It would hurt like hell, but he was certain if he did it right, his plan would work.

Before he reached for the ax, he thought he better check on Raven and Conner and make certain they were both out of commission. An added bump to each of their heads wouldn't make a difference. People always hit their head when they fell.

The house was eerily silent as he made his way to the dark kitchen. He stood at the edge of the hole in the floor and shined his light down. Raven lay down there. She was on her stomach and must have landed on her face. The bright light of his flashlight reflected off the black shine of her hair. Bags of chips lay scattered about her.

It appeared she wouldn't be getting up any time soon, for which Jax was glad. The cellar had been the scariest part of the house for him. The entire time he'd been down there working on removing the stairs, he had heard footsteps on the floors above him. Twice he'd come up to check out who might be in the house with him. Twice he'd found no one.

Conner was the one who worried him. Yes, Jax removed four stairs from the center of the open cellar steps, and truth be told, removing only one would have been enough to cause a person to stumble down the stairs. But Jax didn't doubt for a second, Conner would have pulled his phone from his pocket and turned on the flashlight before taking a step. Of the group, Conner was the thinker. He questioned things. He had questioned the legend of the haunted Devlin Mansion.

Jax opened the small door that led to the steps going down to the cellar. He shined his light down, and, like Raven, found Conner lying face down at the bottom of the stairs.

For a long moment, Jax stood there, staring and contemplating his next move. Conner's right leg was at an odd angle. It was obviously broken. Even if Conner wasn't dead and managed to wake up, Jax doubted he could crawl back up the stairs. And if he could crawl up a few stairs, there was a huge gap where stairs were missing. Even well and unbroken, a typical person might have difficulty managing the three-foot climb.

He let out a heavy breath and moved back out to the candle-lit foyer. He thought he'd feel better having these people out of his life. He thought he'd, at least, feel some satisfaction at having four of his enemies fall into the traps he'd set.

Yet, he felt nothing.

He decided not to wait until midnight to call 9-1-1, but he had a few traps to fix so the cops didn't question him. He stepped over Jason and hiked up the stairs two at a time. When he reached the trip wire he'd stretched across a step, he pulled out the knife and pliers from his back pocket. Once he removed all the evidence, he crammed the fishing line that he'd used for a trip wire into the front pocket of his jeans.

Upstairs, he moved into each bedroom. His dad was a carpenter. All Jax's life, he'd been taught how to use power tools. He'd been taught how to cut and how to repair. The holes he'd cut into the floor in the last two bedrooms had been done with lots of time and great care so he could carefully place the cut-out piece back into the floor. He'd assumed any young woman going up here to screw around with someone would not take the first room for fear of everyone in the party checking out the first room, and he'd been right. Avery had passed up all the rooms.

He started in the last room on the left where he'd hidden his power drill. After placing the cut-out piece back into place, he secured it with four screws. People might think the wood in this place would be rotten, but as a carpenter's son, he knew it was in great shape. Without his help, there would have been no way anyone would fall through the floor.

As he finished placing the last screw to repair the second hole, he again thought he heard a child's giggle. He paused to listen. The sound came from the little girl's bedroom, the one with dolls and the dollhouse in it.

As soon as he finished with the job, he headed back toward the stairs. He checked out all the other rooms on his way.

At the little girl's room, he actually stepped in and shined his light around. There was no one. Obviously, the sound was nothing more than the wind whistling through the eaves or something. There definitely was no one else in the house with him.

He shined his light on the dollhouse. And his breath caught in his chest.

The dolls were no longer in the upstairs bedroom or the kitchen as they were previously.

Now, two dolls lay in the foyer. Two dolls lay in the cellar.

The fifth doll sat at the dining room table.

Avery and Jason must have moved them. There was no other explanation. No one else had been upstairs.

Jax forced himself to breathe.

He needed to end this. He needed to get out of this house.

But first, for some reason he didn't understand, he needed to see the dining room. Earlier in the day, when he'd come to make a plan, cut holes, and create traps, he'd walked through the dining room once just to see if cutting a hole in the floor in that room would be better than a hole in the floor in the kitchen.

He left the hole in the kitchen. He couldn't very well say Raven fell through the floor if there was no hole in the floor. He used the ax to chop away a few bits so it looked as if the old wood broke beneath her weight. He couldn't very well leave it to look as if it had been cut with a power saw.

He shined his light down at her through the hole one last time.

Had her arm been stretched out at that angle when he'd spied her previously?

He couldn't remember and no longer cared.

Very soon, he was going to have cut himself with an ax. The idea wasn't exactly scary, the action was, after all, part of his plan. But it was still going to take some psyching up on his part to do it.

First, he set the ax down and stepped into the dining room.

He stopped inside the door, amazed. Obviously, Raven had been hard at work in this room.

Candle light from the two three-candle candelabras that graced the table lit up the entire room with an inviting, although flickering, glow. The table was set for five, complete with what looked like glass dishes. And Jax swore he smelled roast beef cooking.

He turned and let out a startled gasp at the sight of a woman standing behind him.

"What that—" Jax's heart raced in his chest and felt as if it somehow moved to his throat where it choked him.

"Dinner's almost ready, Sir," the woman said. "We'll need for you to be staying."

Then as he stared, she vanished.

"Shit," he let out.

He turned, having every intention of racing out the front door.

Forget injuring himself for the police, forget staging something else. He had just come face to face with a real ghost. Never mind he was starving, and she mentioned dinner, or that he smelled what smelled like it would be delicious. He didn't want or need to deal with any ghost. Nor did he need to eat with one. He could grab a burger on his way home.

Not while being trapped within the walls of a real haunted house. He didn't like the way she told him he needed to stay, either.

He ran into the kitchen and stopped.

The kitchen was no longer dark, cold, dusty, lacking in counters, or filled with cobwebs.

It was lit bright with lamps and a roaring fire in the hearth. The woman who had just told him dinner was almost ready stood at one of the two butcher blocks arranging a roast, carrots and potatoes onto a platter. She looked up and met his gaze. And smiled a smile that turned his heart cold.

"We love to have guests for dinner," she said. "Plan to stay."

He took a step backwards. Then another.

The impact of landing on the earthen floor of the cellar knocked the wind out of him. And it took him a full five seconds to realize he'd fallen through one of his own traps—the hole in the kitchen floor.

The realization that came to him three seconds after that, when he managed to suck in a much-needed breath, was he didn't land on Raven who had been laying down there. When he attempted to move, a bullet of white, hot pain shot from his left ankle clear out the top of his head causing him to scream out. He looked around trying to see Raven in the shadows. He'd let go of his flashlight in the fall. Using only one leg, and doing his best to keep the injured leg as unmoving as possible, he half crawled to the shadow he recognized as his flashlight that rolled out of reach. He was forced to smack it two times to get everything to connect so it worked. In a huff, he let out the breath he'd been holding as his light lit up the cellar.

Jax vowed when he got out of this dark, musty house, he would keep the lights on all the time.

He was still surprised he didn't see Raven anywhere, but he put that concern on the back burner of his brain. First and foremost, he needed to get out of the cellar. He knew the stairs were the only way. And he was determined to not only reach them but he had to climb the gap and reach the door out of the cellar.

Conner was not at the bottom of the stairs where Jax had seen him lying previously. In fact, there was no sign of anyone having been there. There were no prints or disruptions in the earthen floor. He realized then, too, that not only did he not land on an unconscious Raven, but the box of snacks was gone, too.

He couldn't worry about it now. He needed to get the hell out of the cellar, needed to get out of the house. His leg was on fire as he dragged himself toward the cellar stairs. It didn't help that his flashlight blinked off and on. He continuously was forced to pause and slap it against his hand or the floor to make a connection and have some light.

The destroyed stairs suddenly loomed out of the darkness before him, appearing to be a mountain he wouldn't under normal circumstances want to attempt. Now, however, he had no choice. He attempted to haul himself to a standing position using only his unbroken leg. Despite managing to keep his weight off his injured leg, the motion sent a shot of pain through his body and out the top of his head once again. The pain was so strong, he couldn't help but cry out. Breathing heavily and standing on an uninjured, although wobbling left leg, he managed to grasp the last step before the space where he'd cut out the steps. Had it only been hours before that he'd used his dad's power saw to remove the four steps? It seemed as if it had been an eternity ago.

He hung on to the step as if it was a life ring in an ocean of swells. Jax set his flashlight on the step above him because he found he needed both hands to hoist himself up onto the last floating step. Dragging his injured leg, he managed to pull himself up onto the step. He sucked in deep breath after deep breath for a long moment to avoid vomiting. He was sure his face was on fire and the rest of his body was already burning. He worked to move up the first step. With his clumsy action, he brushed his hand against his flashlight, sending it rolling. With a slight thumping sound, it rolled off the stairs before he could catch it, and it landed soundlessly on the earthen floor where the light went out and left him completely in the dark.

The dark threatened to swallow him, and for a long moment, Jax couldn't breathe beyond it. He closed his eyes against it, and the darkness behind his eyelids was easier to face. He forced in a breath, which filled him with more pain and left him thinking perhaps his chest might explode. The second breath was easier.

He knew there were four steps to the small door that led out into the foyer. With his eyes closed, he forced himself to cover them, his heart feeling as if it tried to pound out of the front of his chest. His hand landed on what he recognized as the door handle, which he, himself, had rigged to come off when Conner tried to open it. He put the handle into the front pocket of his jeans, glad he'd thought to do it. He would be locked in when he reached the top step.

Hopefully, he'd be able to slide the handle in and it would be enough to open the latch.

Otherwise, he'd be locked in forever, which was what he planned for Conner.

He reached the landing.

Finally.

He leaned against the panel of the door and rested on the landing, breathing as if he'd run a marathon. The pain in his leg was unlike anything he'd ever experienced. No matter what he tried, he couldn't even diminish it, and there was no comfortable position.

He pulled the door handle out of his pocket, being extra careful not to drop it, knowing full well there was no way he could venture down and get it if he did. From his—kind of—seated position on the landing, he could reach the hole where the door handle would go. In the dark, with only his hands to feel, he managed to slide the door handle back into place and thought finally, something easy, this better damned well work.

He pulled on the handle.

It did work, the latch opened. The door, thankfully, opened out. It swung open away from him and he, more or less, fell into the candle-lit foyer once again.

The light was so wonderful.

He decided right then, he would never again be in the dark.

He wasn't certain he could drive with his leg in the shape it was in, but he was going to make it work. After he dragged himself out the front door.

He looked up toward the loft landing and saw the broken rungs of the rail where he suspected Avery had crashed through. But Avery was no longer lying in the foyer. Jason wasn't lying at the bottom of the stairs.

There were no puddles of blood to indicate they'd even been there, either. What the hell? Was he losing his damned mind?

Jax didn't know where the others were, or what became of them, and he didn't care. He couldn't believe they'd managed to leave on their own accord, or clean up the messes left by their blood. He was pretty sure he would have heard some sort of sound indicating such. Maybe the ghosts took them and was forcing them to stay for dinner.

The chuckle he let out at that thought was loud and sounded foreign to his own ears. He didn't allow himself to time to think about his so-called friends. He needed to escape. The sounds of his body sliding across the dusty floor as he dragged himself toward the front door were loud and odd, too. He would have expected them to echo, but they didn't.

Being prone, with his injured leg dragging behind him, proved to be the best-feeling position for it since he'd landed on it. Pulling himself toward the door was the easiest thing he'd managed in the past hour. With every reach of his hands and pull of his body, he drew closer to freedom.

Tears of joy sprang to his eyes as he reached the door. Escape from this horrid house was within reach, so close he thought he could taste it.

And in less than a heartbeat, it was swiped away from him. He let out a fearful, frustrated cry as he felt the hands of an unseen person who suddenly grasped him by both of his ankles and slid him across the floor back toward the door that led to the cellar. The motion sent a fresh wave of burning pain through his leg. He screamed against it. Then he looked over his shoulder and screamed louder as true horror grasped him and sent ice into his soul.

It was the ghost cook who grasped the back of his ankles.

The evil smile on her face seemed to shimmer and was filled with satisfaction. "There is no leaving. As I told you, supper will be served shortly."

Jax wasn't even sure how he managed to hear her vibrating words over his own screams and above his pain.

Motion caught his eye as the front door opened. A stranger stood there, a man, looking taller than tall, his face hidden in the shadows. "No!"

His no also wasn't as loud as Jax's screams, yet Jax heard it.

The cook stopped her motion of dragging him. She released him, dropping his injured leg against the floor with a sickening plop. He groaned against the pain.

"He disrupted our home, actually destroyed parts of our home. He should be forced to remain in the mess he created." The cook's words vibrated and reminded him of when he was a kid and he talked pressing his mouth against an electric fan.

"No," the stranger said again. "He comes with me."

The authority in the stranger's voice was comforting. Jax would never argue against that authority. He hoped the fucking ghost couldn't, either. Jax tried to slither away from the ghost cook. He glanced back just in time to see her lift her foot and stomp on his hurt leg. He cried out against the pain. He didn't try to comprehend how a phantom could grab him, lift his leg, or stomp on him. He was too busy working to think beyond the new level of pain her action had brought to him.

"Are you considering stepping back into this house?" the cook asked the stranger. "We let you and the others leave once. Do you think we'll be so generous to allow anyone to escape again?"

"I am going to step inside. And I'm going to help Jax out of here. You will not stop me."

The cook laughed, and the sound seemed to shudder through the foyer. "I might not stop you. But she will."

The ghost woman indicated toward the stairs where there was a figure between Jax's savior and him. It was a child ghost, a little girl. She held Jax's ax. She giggled. "It's going to be so exciting to have a new face at the table for dinner!"

Jax recognized the sound of that giggle. He'd heard it when he'd been hidden in the small space near the stairs. It had been that killer child ghost who had called him to come out from his hiding place. She now wielded his ax, a real ax. The grin on her face was that of pure evil.

"I want him to stay. We can play a forever game of Hide and Seek," the child said. Her voice vibrated as the cook's had.

Before Jax could comprehend what was happening, the stranger at the door yelled, "No!"

The child raised the ax.

Jax was allowed only a single heartbeat of thought to realize the little girl ghost meant to bring the ax down on him.

He screamed, anticipating more pain. Anticipating death, as he felt his heart racing in his throat.

At the last possible moment, he was dragged across the floor out of the way, out of the reach of the ax.

The blade collided with the tile of the floor, filling the entire foyer with a bong sound that was louder than any bell. It left his head ringing as a high-pitched buzz filled his hearing. A slight gust of air from the motion of the ax touched his arm. He had been saved by the stranger, who had leapt into the room, grabbed his arms and slid him out of the way.

The stranger dragged him as the cook had, although, now by his arms, and not his injured leg, but he was slid across the dusty floor toward the front door. The little girl sliced the ax through the air again and caught the stranger on his forearm before he managed to move out of the way. The man let out painful grunt but paused only slightly in his efforts to pull Jax to the safety of the front door.

As the little ghost raised the ax again, the stranger completely stopped in his pulling action and stood up straight. Jax yelled for him not to stop, please don't stop.

To Jax's surprise, the man pulled out what appeared to be gun. Would a gun even work on a ghost? Before he could question the thought, the man pulled the trigger and what appeared to be a spray of crystals hit the child square in the chest. She shimmered, screamed and vanished. The ax tumbled to the floor with a clunking noise.

In the next second, the cook who was now a short distance from Jax's feet screamed, "You—" It was all she managed to get out before the stranger shot her, too, and she vanished.

The stranger moved away from him, sending Jax into a panic. "No! Don't leave me here."

"I'm not, but there isn't much time." He reached the ax. "We can't let them have this." He slung it away and out the front door, where Jax heard noises of it cartwheeling on the wood of the porch. Then the stranger once again reached for him. This time, Jax held out his hands, and the man took them.

Jax found the man's hands to be warm and comforting. With the stranger stepping backward and pulling Jax, they reached the front door. The cool, fall air touched him, and Jax breathed it in, feeling like a marathon runner crossing the finish line.

Then he felt the touch of hands grab his ankles again and he yelled out. The grip was strong. The stranger who held his hands was stopped so suddenly, he lost his grip and fell backwards, landing out the open front door on his butt.

"No!" Jax cried out as he felt the motion of being dragged back into the foyer. Another shot rang out as the stranger fired his gun again from his seated position. Whoever or whatever grasped his ankles was gone.

Then the guy grabbed a hold of him again and hauled him out the front door into the night air. As soon as Jax's entire body was on the porch, the stranger slammed the front door.

Jax rested against one of the posts.

His nameless savior breathed heavily, too, but he didn't pause to rest or catch his breath. Instead, he reached for a duffle bag that rested nearby. From inside, he took out a chain which he looped through the double handles of the two front doors. He secured the chain by sliding a padlock through the links of the chain and bolting it closed.

"Who are you?" Jax asked.

"I'm a cop. You can call me Tony." Then Tony looked toward the far end of the porch where Jax had left his pickup truck parked beside the car his friends had driven—the very one he'd sabotaged in case any of them escaped his traps.

"Come over here and help me," the cop called out.

Jason and Conner appeared at the far end of the porch.

Jax had no idea how they could be alive, or at least up and walking, but they were.

"If what you say is true, he tried to kill us. So why should we do anything for him?" Conner asked

Tony paused and stared at them. "Because I asked you to. Besides, I'm tired, I'm hungry, and I'm bleeding. If you don't, I'll arrest you for obstruction."

Tony looked as tired as Jax felt, and blood seeped through the sleeve of the hoodie he wore. Jax wasn't sure Tony could stop Conner or Jason if either of them chose to turn tail and run. He would never know, because in the end, Jason and Connor helped Jax to his truck. Sitting in the front seat put pressure on his broken leg. He bit his lip against complaining about it or even groaning. The pain, although horrible, was still better than being left in that house. Tony stood outside the open driver side door of Jax's truck and wrapped a rolled bandage around his own arm. He tied it off with his teeth and reminded Jax of an Army field medic. Jax heard the others start their car and a moment later, the sound of the engine faded into the dark as they drove away. He didn't know where the others went or how they got their car to start, and the cop didn't give him any clues.

Tony didn't even ask him how he felt; he just drove Jax to the hospital.

And left him there.

When Jax awoke the next morning after surgery to repair his broken leg with a plate and six screws, he found himself alone.

And none of the nurses knew anything about any cop named Tony.

~ ~ ~ ~ ~

Detective Tony Grayson stepped out onto his second story balcony where Sara Greene sat in one of the two rocking chairs and waited. He closed the sliding glass door. He leaned down and kissed her tenderly. The touch of her lips grounded him and calmed him as nothing else ever had. Then he sank into the second empty rocking chair beside her. On the table between them was a charcuterie board of breakfast foods—sausage, sugar bacon, triangles of buttered wheat toast, a plate of scrambled eggs, and two small bowls of maple syrup.

"Your coffee is hot," she said.

He took a sip, and followed it with a deep breath, filling his lungs with cool, early morning air. "Thank you." He picked up a piece of toast and sampled a small bite, chewing it carefully, uncertain what his stomach could handle after the stitches.

"How many stitches did you get?" she asked.

"Eighteen on the outside." He took another sip of coffee, allowing it to flow through his gut and warm him. He realized then he'd been cold since the moment he woke from his dream and left Sara in their bed, to go save a group of thoughtless college kids. The toast seemed to settle where it should, so he took another bite.

"And?"

"And six on the inside," he confessed.

"And you got your tetanus shot?"

"Absolutely."

Sara let out a relieved sigh. "And did you manage to save all five?"

"Yes, although the four he lured there to kill wanted me to leave him, but I couldn't."

She smiled over at him. "That isn't who you are, don't say it like it's a bad thing."

He looked out over the waking town of Mossy Point. Justin Anderston, the postal carrier walked down the street carrying his bag filled with mail. The sun peeked out, casting orange on the dish of syrup. "I can't even charge him. That would require an investigation, which would require sending others—more possible victims—into that house. I can't let that happen. I can't ever let anyone venture into that place. And since there can't be an investigation with someone confirming the traps he set, it would be his word against theirs, something a damned good lawyer could nip in the bud."

"I know," Sara replied softly.

"So, he gets away with it." It was more a statement than a question.

"Does he?" she asked.

"Not really, I guess," Tony confirmed. "First, it's going to take some time and lots of physical therapy for him to walk again. Then he's going to limp for the rest of his natural life and probably have pain when it rains, both of which will be constant reminders. And even when he does finally heal, I'm sure he's not going to be able to sit in class with any of the four people he wanted to leave there dead, which means his college career, at least here, is over." He used one of the two forks placed on the board to take a bite of eggs.

Sara dipped a pancake into the syrup and ate it, careful to not drip any.

Tony set his coffee mug back on the small table and absently rubbed his head above his right brow, working to press away the headache he felt trying to start there. "The ghosts...the evil of that place...the ghosts were so strong, they could grab that kid. They could swing a real ax."

Sara gently placed her hand on his arm below the bandage that covered his stitched skin. "Don't. You managed to be stronger, that's what's important."

He met her gaze. "It makes me afraid to go back to sleep."

"Me, too. How do you think this works."

He took her hand. "I think for us, this is working great."

"No, I mean the dreams. Do you think we'll keep sharing them? And dreaming about whoever needs help?"

Tony shrugged. "I suppose you'll just have to keep sleeping beside me, holding my hand to see."

"Maybe I could go with you sometime and help with whatever it is you see in our dream."

"Maybe," Tony said, although he had no intention of letting her go if things were going to be like the evil he just escaped. He could never let the woman who held his heart be that close to anything so evil.

"Do you think that ghost child really killed her entire family?" Sara asked.

"I don't know. But I want to show you something." Tony pulled out his phone.

"What?"

"I managed to take a picture. There wasn't much time, but there was just something so off about the dining room where the table was set for dinner. I took a picture of it." Tony opened the photo app on his phone and pulled one up. "Look at this."

Sara took his phone and looked. "Are you sure one of those college kids didn't set the table?"

"Look at the mirror at the end of the room."

Sara did and gasped.

In the mirror's reflection, the table was set just as it was in real time. Yet in the reflection, five ghostly figures sat in the chairs, one at each set place.

Other books by Allie Harrison

Small Town Secrets
Small Town Storm
Small Town Graveyard
Hargrove House
Montgomery Manor
Camden Place
Winsgate Drive
Invisible
Unafraid
Initiation
Bad Medicine
No Fear
Hide and Seek

ABOUT THE AUTHOR

Allie Harrison lives in Southern Illinois. She enjoys writing urban fantasy, thrillers, horror, suspense, and paranormal, whatever it takes to keep the reader on the edge of the seat. When she isn't writing or searching out her next hero or favorite setting, she stays busy with her family. If she doesn't answer her phone, she's probably out hiking, camping, biking, reading something fun, or cooking up something unique. You can find her at:

Facebook:https://www.facebook.com/Allie-Harrison-Author-106928505995715/

Twitter: https://twitter.com/ImAllieHarrison

Website http://www.allieharrison.com